continued . . .

Drinking Midnight Wine

"[Simon R. Green] . . . offers another wildly fantastic extravaganza."
—Publishers Weekly

"A trip worth taking. Green weaves numerous plot threads together with vivid characters, sharp dialogue, and a touch of Terry Pratchettish absurdity."
—Booklist

"An engaging cross-world fantasy that transforms a small English village into a realm of wonder and nightmare."
—Library Journal

Beyond the Blue Moon

"Continuing the adventures of a pair of charmingly roguish and intensely honorable heroes, this fast-moving, wisecracking [novel] belongs in most fantasy collections."
—Library Journal

"As always Green provides plenty of spectacular violence and some spectacular wonders."
—Locus

"What makes this novel stand out among its numerous peers is the lead characters whose love and commitment to one another in the midst of epic escapades keeps them grounded in humanity."
—Midwest Book Review

NIGHTINGALE'S LAMENT

SIMON R. GREEN

ACE BOOKS, NEW YORK

NIGHTINGALE'S LAMENT

An Ace Book / published by arrangement with
the author

PRINTING HISTORY
Ace mass market edition / May 2004

ISBN: 978-0-441-01163-6

ACE®
Ace Books are published by The Berkley Publishing Group,
a division of Penguin Group (USA) Inc.,
375 Hudson Street, New York, New York 10014.
ACE and the "A" design
are trademarks belonging to Penguin Group (USA) Inc.

PRINTED IN THE UNITED STATES OF AMERICA

20   19   18   17   16   15   14   13   12

My name is John Taylor. I've made that a name to be respected and feared, but it's also made me a target my whole life.

I operate as a private eye, in a world where gods and monsters are real. The Nightside: the sick, secret magical heart of London. A place where dreams come true, whether you want them to or not. It's not easy to find a way in, and it can be even harder to find a way out.

I can find anything, solve any mystery. Except the answers to the dark and deadly secrets of my own past.

My name is John Taylor. And if you've come looking for me, either you're in trouble, or you're about to be.

ONE

The Hanged Man's Beautiful Daughter

There are all kinds of Powers running loose in the Nightside, but its power sources have to be rather more reliable, as well as completely divorced from outside interference. Someone's got to pump out the electricity to keep all that hot neon burning. The Nightside, being a city within a city, draws its energies from many sources—some of them illegal, some of them unnatural. Power is generated by blood sacrifices and imprisoned godlings, gestalt minds and tiny black holes held captive inside stasis fields. And there are other sources, so vast and awful, so alien and unutterably *other*, that just to glimpse their secret workings would drive a man insane. Not that anyone cares about such things in the Nightside, not as long as the lights are bright and the trains keep running. But the only really dependable source for *electricity* used to be the futuristic power plant of Prometheus Inc. Magic may be more flashy, but there's always been as much super-science as sorcery in the Nightside.

Prometheus Inc. was a fairly recent success story. Not quite six years old, it had a reputation for dependability and savagely undercutting prices, which made it the company that supplied some twelve per cent of the Nightside's electricity. So the recent sudden outbreak of sabotage and destruction inside the closely guarded power plant could not be allowed to continue. Walker made that very clear. Walker represents the Authorities, the shadowy people who run things here, inasmuch as anyone does, or can. He sends the occasional job my way, when it suits him, because I am quiet, dependable, and entirely expendable.

I stood in the shadows at the end of the street, quietly studying the hulking edifice that was Prometheus Inc. It wasn't much to look at—just another great tower block of glass and steel. The top floors were offices, administration and the like. Middle floors were laboratories, for research and development. And the bottom floor was public relations. The power plant itself, that modern wonder of efficiency and incredible output, was supposedly somewhere underground. I say supposedly, because as far as I knew, only a handful of people had ever seen it. The whole thing was automated, run from a single control centre, and even after six years no-one had any idea of what it was or how it worked. And it's not easy, keeping secrets in the Nightside.

The whole Prometheus Inc. success story had happened while I was away, trying—and failing—to live an ordinary life in the ordinary world. Now I was back, and I was quite keen to see what was being hidden under the surface of Prometheus Inc. I like knowing things that no-one else does. It's helped me keep alive, down the years. I strolled out of the shadows and headed for the office building. There was a small army of security men and rent-a-cops surrounding the place, and those nearest the main door lifted their heads and paid attention as they spotted me approaching. An awful lot of guns zeroed in on me, and the sound of safeties clicking off was almost deafening. If I'd been anyone else, I might have been worried.

I came to a halt before the main door and smiled at the rent-a-cops arrayed before me, in their wonderfully striking uniforms of midnight blue with silver piping. I nodded to the officer in charge, a tall and somewhat overweight man with cold, careful eyes. He held his ground, and his gaze didn't waver, though behind him we could both hear his men whispering my name. Some of them crossed themselves or made ancient warding signs. I let my smile widen just a little, because I could see it upset them. Ever since I tracked down the Unholy Grail and stood off two armies of angels to do it, my reputation had been going through the roof. Mostly nonsense, of course, but I did nothing to discourage the rumours, particularly the nasty ones. Nothing like a good—or more properly speaking a bad—reputation to keep the flies off.

"I'm supposed to ask for identification," said the officer. "And shoot anyone who isn't on the approved list."

"You know who I am," I said calmly. "And I'm expected."

The officer relaxed a little. "First good news I've had all night. Hello, Taylor. I'm actually glad to see you. This whole business has my people seriously spooked."

"Has anyone been killed?" I asked, frowning. "I understood this was just a sabotage case."

"No deaths as yet, but a hell of a lot of casualties." The officer scowled. "Whoever's tearing this place apart doesn't give a damn about anyone who gets in his way. I've lost forty of my people in the last three nights, and I still haven't got a clue as to who's behind it all. No-one ever sees anything, until it's too late. I've had this place closed up tighter than a duck's arse, and still the bastard keeps getting in."

"Inside job?" I asked, to show I was paying attention.

"That was my first thought, but there hasn't been anyone in there for a week. The boss sent them all home when the problems started. He's the only one left in the building. I ran the usual security checks on the staff anyway, just in case, but nothing showed up. Most of them haven't been around long enough to work up a serious grudge."

"So what's freaking your men?" I asked quietly. "If they were any more on edge, they'd be shooting each other."

The officer snorted. "I told you. No-one ever sees *anything*. I've got saturation coverage around the building, CCTV inside, and infrared and motion sensors working. And whoever it is comes and goes without setting off any of them."

"There are a lot of things in the Nightside that come and go as they please," I pointed out.

"Don't I know it. But this is supposed to be a high-tech, low-magic area. If any heavy-duty magic-user had appeared here, he'd have set off all kinds of alarms. Whoever or whatever's trying to shut this place down, it's outside anything I've ever experienced, in science or magic."

I nodded easily, doing my best to exude casual confidence. "That's why they sent for me. Because I find the answers other people can't. See you later."

I stepped past the officer and headed for the main door, only to stop abruptly as one of the rent-a-cops moved suddenly forward to block my way. He was a big lad, with muscles on his muscles, and his huge hands made the semi-automatic in his grasp look like a toy. He scowled at me in what he obviously imagined was an intimidating way.

"Everyone gets frisked for guns," he snapped. "That's the rules. No exceptions. Even for jumped-up ambulance chasers like you, Taylor."

The officer started to say something, but I stopped him with a quick gesture. The day I couldn't deal with a constipated rent-a-cop, I'd retire. I gave him my best nasty smile.

"I don't use guns. Never have. They have too many limitations."

I slowly raised my hands, opened them, and the rent-a-cop's eyes widened as a steady stream of bullets fell from my hands to bounce and rattle on the ground at his feet.

"Your gun is empty," I said. "Now get out of my way

before I decide to do something unpleasantly similar to your insides."

He pulled the trigger anyway, and made a small unhappy sound in the back of his throat when nothing happened. He swallowed hard and stepped back. I walked past him as though he didn't exist. I could hear the officer chewing him out as I passed through the heavy main door into the lobby beyond.

I strolled into the luxurious reception area as though I owned the place, but the effect was wasted, because there was no-one there. I heard electronic locks closing behind me. Someone knew I was there. I looked around the lobby and quickly spotted the security cameras tucked away in the ceiling corners. All the little red lights were on, so I just stood there and let the cameras get a good look at me. I thought I looked pretty good. My white trench coat was actually a little cleaner than usual, and I was almost sure I'd remembered to shave. Appearances can be so important. There was a brief burst of static from an unseen speaker, then a familiar voice whispered in the great empty lobby.

"John, I'm so glad you're here. Come on through to the manager's office and join me. Take the blue door at the end of the lobby, and follow the arrows. Don't go wandering. I've got booby-traps set up everywhere. And watch your back. We never know when the saboteur's going to strike next."

I passed through the blue door and followed the glowing arrows that appeared on the wall beyond. After the luxurious reception lobby, the inner workings of Prometheus Inc. turned out to be decidedly functional. Narrow corridors with bare walls, numbered doors, and scuffed carpeting. It was all very quiet, as though the whole building was tense, waiting for something bad to happen. The arrows finally led me to a door with the Prometheus company logo on it, and there waiting to greet me was the manager-owner himself, Vincent Kraemer.

He nodded and smiled and shook my hand, but it was clear his thoughts were somewhere else. The man was seriously worried, and it showed. He ushered me into his office, looked quickly down the corridor, and shut and locked the door. He waved me to the visitor's chair and seated himself behind the magnificent mahogany desk. The office looked comfortable, lived in. Nice prints on the walls, deep deep carpet, and a high-tech drinks cabinet in the corner. All the usual signs of success. But the desk top was covered in papers that had overflowed and almost buried the In and Out trays, and one whole wall of the office was covered in CCTV monitor screens, showing ever-shifting views of the power plant interior. I studied them for a while, to show I was taking an interest, but it was all just machinery to me. I couldn't tell a turbine from a teapot, unless one of them had a tea cosy on it. Everything seemed to be working okay for the moment, and the walkways were deserted. I turned my attention back to the manager, and he flashed me another preoccupied smile.

I knew him vaguely, from several years back. Vincent Kraemer was one of those people who was always running around like a mad thing, trying to put far-fetched and precarious deals into motion, chasing after the one Big Score that would make him horribly wealthy. He finally made it, with Prometheus Inc. Vincent was tall, buff, immaculately dressed, with a prematurely lined face and no hair left to speak of. His suit probably cost more than I used to make in a year.

"Good to see you again, John." His voice was steady, cultivated, and artificially calm. "Been hearing interesting things about you since you got back."

"And you've done very well," I said courteously. "Is wealth and success everything you thought it would be?"

He laughed briefly. "Pretty much. What do you think of my pride and joy, John?"

"Impressive, but I'm not really equipped to appreciate it. Technology has always been a mystery to me. I have to get my secretary to work the timer on my video."

He laughed dutifully. "It's your other areas of expertise I need, John. I need you to find out who's trying to drive me out of business."

And then he stopped, because he saw I was looking at the only photo on his desk. A wedding scene, in a simple silver frame. Bride, groom, best man, and me. Six years ago, and still as fresh in my memory as though it had happened yesterday. It should have been the happiest day in the lives of two wonderful young people, but it instead it became a tragedy that everyone still talked about. Mostly because no-one had ever been found to blame it on.

The bride was Melinda Dusk, also known as the Hanged Man's Beautiful Daughter. The groom was Quinn, also known as the Sunslinger. She wore a wedding gown of brilliant white, with a long creamy train. He wore his best cowboy outfit, all black leathers studded with dazzling displays of steel and silver. And standing on either side of the happy couple, doing our best to look at ease in our rented tuxedos, Vincent Kraemer as best man, and me as the bride's oldest friend. Melinda and Quinn—scions of the two oldest and most powerful families in the Nightside. Married and murdered in the same day.

There aren't many happy endings in the Nightside. Even the greatest celebrities and the most powerful people aren't immune to tragedy. Melinda was of the dark, her powers those of shadow and sorcery. Quinn was of the light, the deadly energies he controlled derived from the power of the sun itself. Their ancestors, the original Hanged Man and the original Sunslinger, had been deadly enemies hundreds of years ago, and all the generations since then had continued the feud, polishing their hatred with years of constant use. And Melinda and Quinn, the two latest avatars in this ongoing struggle, raised to hate and fight each other to the death, happened to meet during one of the rare truces. And it was love at first sight.

They continued to meet in secret for months, but finally went public. Their families went berserk and almost went to war. But Melinda and Quinn stood firm, secure in the powers they wielded, and threatened to disown their families and elope if they weren't given permission to marry. It was a magnificent wedding in the end, attended by absolutely every member of both families, partly as a show of strength and partly to make sure neither side tried to pull a fast one. There were famous faces and celebrities everywhere, and Walker himself turned up to run security. It should have been the safest place in the Nightside.

Vincent and I also worked as ushers, showing people to their seats, frisking them for weapons, keeping everyone in order, always ready to jump on anyone who even looked like doing anything funny. We were both young men then, still building our reputations. They called Vincent the Mechanic, because he could build or fix anything. Magic was good for short cuts, he was fond of saying, but technology was always going to be the more dependable in the long run. He'd built an automatic confetti-thrower, especially for the wedding, and kept dashing off to tinker with it when he wasn't needed. He and Quinn had been friends since they were kids, and he had risked his life many times to act as go-between for the two lovers. Melinda was one of the few friends I had left from childhood, one of the few powerful enough in her own right that my enemies didn't dare mess with her.

The wedding ceremony went fine, the families behaved themselves, and no-one got the words wrong or dropped the ring. And when it was all over, everyone cheered and applauded and some of us dared to think that just maybe the long war was over at last. Bride and groom left the church together, looking radiant. As though they belonged together. As though they completed each other. The automatic confetti-chucker worked first time.

Everyone posed for photographs, drinks circulated, snacks were consumed, and old enemies nodded to each other from a safe distance, even exchanging a few polite words. Bride and groom accepted the bridal cup, full to the brim with the very best champagne, and toasted their families and the bright future ahead. Ten minutes later, they were both dead. Poison in the bridal cup. It was all over so quickly that neither magic nor science could save them. Whoever had chosen the poison had known what they were doing. There wasn't even a sign of symptoms until Quinn suddenly fell dead to the ground. Melinda lived long enough to hold her dead husband in her arms, her tears dropping onto his dead face, then she collapsed across him and was gone.

If Walker and his people hadn't been there, the wedding party would have turned into a massacre. Both families went crazy, blaming each other. Somehow Walker kept the sides separated until they all left, swearing vengeance, then he organised a full investigation, using all his considerable resources. He never found anything. There was no shortage of suspects, of people in both families who'd spoken out loudly against the wedding and the truce, but there was no proof, no evidence. Meanwhile, the two families fought running battles in the streets, mercilessly slaughtering anyone foolish enough to be caught out on their own. Finally, the Authorities stepped in and shut it down, threatening to banish both families from the Nightside. A slow, sullen armed truce prevailed, but only just. That was six years ago. Melinda and Quinn were cold in their separate family graves, and still no-one had any idea of the who or why of it. There are loads of conspiracy theories, but then, there always are.

I would have done my best to find the killer, but shortly after the wedding my own life went to hell in a hurry, and I ended up running from the Nightside with Suzie Shooter's bullet in my back, vowing never to return.

"Such a terrible tragedy," said Vincent. He picked up the photo and studied it. "I still miss them. Like part of me died with them. Sometimes I think I keep this photo on my desk as a reminder of the last time I was really

happy." He put the photo down and smiled briefly at
me. "I wish they could have seen this place. My greatest achievement. And now someone, or something, is
trying to shut it down. Which is why I asked Walker to
contact you, John. Can you help me?"

"Perhaps," I said. "I'm still trying to get a feel for
what's going on here. Talk me through it, from the beginning."

Vincent leaned back in his manager's chair and
linked his fingers together across his expansive waist-
coat. While he talked, his voice was calm and even, but
his gaze kept flickering to the CCTV monitors.

"It started two weeks ago, John. Everything normal,
just another day. Until one of the main turbines suddenly stopped working. My people investigated and
found it had been sabotaged. Not a professional job—
the whole interior had simply been . . . ripped apart.
My people repaired it and got it back on-line in under
an hour, but by then systems were breaking down all
through the plant. And that's been the pattern ever
since. As fast as we fix things, something else goes
wrong. It's costing us a fortune in spare parts alone.
There's nothing sophisticated about the sabotage, just
brutal, senseless destruction.

"No-one ever sees the saboteur. You've seen the security I've hired, but they haven't made a blind bit of
difference. I've got cameras everywhere, and they
never see anything either. I've had the videotapes
checked by experts, but there's no trace of anything.
We can't even tell how the bastard gets in or out! The
destruction's getting steadily worse. Repairs and recon-
struction are starting to fall behind. It's only a matter of
time before it starts affecting our power output. And a

whole lot of people depend on the electricity we produce here."

And if Prometheus Inc. goes down, so do you, I
thought, but I was still being polite, so I didn't say it
aloud.

"How about rivals?" I said. "Perhaps someone in the
same line of business, looking to profit at your expense?"

"There are always competitors," said Vincent,
frowning. "But there's no-one else big enough to take
over if we go under. Prometheus Inc. supplies 12.4 per
cent of the Nightside's electricity needs. If we crash,
there'll be power outages and brownouts all across the
Nightside, and no-one wants that. The other companies
would have to push themselves almost to destruction to
take up the slack."

"All right," I said. "How about people who just
don't like you? Made any new enemies recently?"

He smiled briefly. "A month ago, I would have said
I didn't have an enemy in the world. But now . . ." He
looked at the wedding photo on his desk again. "I've
been having dreams . . . about Melinda and Quinn, and
the day they died. And I have to wonder . . . if the bastard who killed them is coming after me."

I hadn't seen that twist coming. "Why you? And
why wait six years?"

"Maybe the killer thinks I know something, though
I'm damned if I know what. And just maybe it's all
started up again because you're back, John. An awful
lot of old grudges and feuds have bubbled to the surface since you returned to the Nightside."

He had a point there, so I decided to change the subject. "Let's talk about the actual damage here. You said it was . . . unsophisticated."

"Hell yes," said Vincent. "It's clear the saboteur has no real technical knowledge. There are a dozen places he could have hit that would shut the whole plant down if they were even interfered with. But none a layman could hope to recognise. And, of course, there's the secret process at the heart of Prometheus Inc. that makes this whole operation possible. I invented it. But that's kept inside a steel vault, protected by state-of-the-art high-tech defence systems. Even the Authorities would have a hard time getting to it without the right pass codes." Vincent leaned forward across the desk and fixed me with a pleading gaze. "You've got to help me, John. It's not only my livelihood we're talking about here. If Prometheus Inc. is forced off-line, and power levels drop all across the Nightside, people are going to start dying. Hundreds of thousands of lives could be at risk."

I should have seen what was coming. But I always was a sucker for a sob story.

Vincent took me on a tour through the plant, the underground section that outsiders never got a chance to see. It was all spotlessly clean and eerily quiet. The actual generators themselves turned out to be much smaller than I expected, and made hardly a sound. There were panels and gauges and readouts and any amount of gleaming high tech, none of which meant anything to me, though I was careful to make impressed sounds at regular intervals. Every bit of it had been designed by Vincent, back when he was the Mechanic, rather than the Manager. He kept up a running commentary throughout the tour, most of which went right over my head, while I nodded and smiled and kept an eye out for the saboteur. Eventually Vincent ran out of things to point at, and we stopped at the end of a cavernous hall, before a large, closed, solid steel door. He looked at me, clearly expecting me to say something.

"It's all . . . very clean," I said. "And very impressive. Though it's hard to believe you produce so much of the Nightside's electricity with . . . just this. I was expecting something ten times the size."

Vincent grinned. "None of the power comes from *this*. All the machinery does is convert the power produced in there into electricity. The secret lies in my own special process, behind this sealed door. A scientific marvel, if I do say so myself."

I glared suddenly at the steel door. "If you're about to tell me you've got a nuclear pile in there . . ."

"No, no . . ."

"Or a contained singularity . . ."

"Nothing so crude, John. My process is perfectly safe, with no noxious by-products. Though I'm afraid I can't show it to you. Some things have to remain secret."

And then he broke off, and we both looked round sharply as we heard something. A harsh juddering began in one of the machines at the far end of the hall, and black smoke billowed suddenly from a vent, before an alarm shrilled loudly and the machine shut itself down. Vincent shrank back against the steel door.

"He's here! The saboteur . . . he's never got this far before. He must have been following us all this time . . . Are you armed, John?"

"I don't use guns," I said. "I've never felt the need."

"Normally I don't, either, but ever since this shit began happening, I've felt a lot more secure knowing I've got a little something to even out the odds." Vincent produced a gleaming silver gun from inside his jacket. It looked sleek and deadly and very futuristic. Vincent hefted it proudly. "It's a laser. Amplified light to fight the forces of darkness. Another of my inventions. I always meant to do more with it, but the power plant took over my life. I can't see anyone, John. Can you see anyone?"

A machine a little further down the hall exploded suddenly. More black smoke, and the hum of the other machines rose significantly, as though they were having to work harder. A third machine blew apart like a grenade, throwing sharp-edged steel shrapnel almost the length of the hall. Some of the overhead lights flickered and went out. There were shadows everywhere now, deep and dark. Some of the other machines began making unpleasant, threatening noises. And still there was no sign of the saboteur anywhere.

Vincent's face was pale and sweaty, and his hand trembled as he swept his laser gun back and forth, searching for a target. "Come on, come on," he said hoarsely. "You're on my territory now. I'm ready for you."

Something pale flashed briefly at the corner of my eye. I snapped around, but it was already gone. It appeared again, just a glimpse of white in the shadows between two machines. It flashed back and forth, appearing and disappearing in the blink of an eye, darting up and down the length of the hall. Glimmers of shimmering white as fleeting as moonlight, but I thought I was beginning to make out an impression of a pale, haunted face. It moved in the shadows, never venturing out into the light. But it was gradually drawing nearer. Heading for us, or perhaps for the steel door behind us and the secret vulnerable heart of Prometheus Inc.

My first thought was that it had to be a ghost of some kind, maybe a poltergeist. Which would explain why the CCTV cameras hadn't been able to see anything. Ghosts could operate in science- or magic-dominated areas, provided their motivation was strong enough. In which case, Vincent needed a priest or an exorcist, not a private eye. I suggested as much to Vincent, and he shrugged angrily.

"I had my people do a full background check on this location before we began construction; and they didn't turn up anything. The whole area was supposed to be entirely free from magical or paranormal influences. That's why I built here. I'm the Mechanic, I build things. It's a talent, just like your talent for finding things, John. I don't know about ghosts. You're the expert on these matters. What do we do?"

"Depends what the ghost wants," I said.

"It wants to destroy me! I would have thought that was obvious. *What was that?*"

The white figure was flashing in and out of the shadows, on every side at once, drawing steadily closer all the time. Shimmering white, ragged round the edges, with long, reaching arms and a dark malevolent glare in an indistinct face. It gestured abruptly, and suddenly all the shrapnel scattered across the floor rose and hammered us like a metallic hailstorm. I put my arms over my head and did my best to shield Vincent with my body. The rain of objects ended as suddenly as it began, and we looked up to see something pale and dangerous squatting on one of the machines, tearing it apart with unnatural strength. Vincent howled with rage and fired his laser, but the figure was gone long before the light beam could reach it. I glared about me, my back pressed hard against the steel door. There were no other exits, no way to escape. So I did the only thing I could. I used my talent.

I don't like to use it too often, or for too long. It helps my enemies find me.

I reached inside, concentrating, and my third eye, my private eye, slowly opened. And just like that, I could see her clearly. As though my psychic gaze had focussed her, made her plain at last, she walked out of the shadows and into the light, standing openly before us. She nodded to me, then glared at Vincent with her deep dark eyes. I knew her immediately, though she looked very different from her wedding photo. Melinda Dusk, dead these six years, still wearing her wonderful white wedding dress, though it hung in tatters about her corpse-pale body. Her raven black hair fell in thick ringlets to her bare shoulders. Her lips were a pale purple. Her eyes . . . were black on black, like two deep holes in her face. She looked angry, haunted, vicious. The Hanged Man's Daughter, mistress of the dark forces, still beautiful in a cold, unnatural way. She raised one hand to point accusingly at Vincent, her fingernails grown long in the grave. I glanced at Vincent. He was breathing fast, his whole body trembling, but he didn't look particularly surprised.

I shut down my talent, but she was still there. I took a step forward, and the ghost turned her awful unblinking gaze upon me. I held up my hands to show they were empty.

"Melinda," I said. "It's me, John."

She looked away. I wasn't important. All her attention, all her rage, was focussed on Vincent.

"Talk to me, Vincent," I said quietly. "What's going on here? You knew who and what it was all along, didn't you? Didn't you! Why is she so angry with you, angry enough to pull her up out of her grave after six years?"

"I didn't know," he said. "I swear I didn't know!"

"He knew," said Melinda. Her voice was clear but quiet, like a whisper in my ear, as though it had to travel impossible distances to reach me. "You chose this place well, Vincent. As far as you could get from my family plot, and still be in the Nightside. And the sacrifices you made here in secret, before construction began, the innocent blood you spilled, and the promises you made . . . they would have kept out anyone else but me. I am an avatar of the dark, and every shadow is a doorway to me. Six years it took me, to track you down. But you could never hope to keep me out, not when the only thing that matters to me is still here. I will have my revenge, Vincent. Dear good friend Vincent. For what you did, to me and to Quinn."

And that was when I finally understood. I looked at Vincent, too shocked even to be angry, for the moment.

"You killed them," I said. "You murdered Melinda and Quinn. But you were their friend . . ."

"Best friends," said Vincent. He'd stopped shaking, and his voice was steady. "I would have done anything for you two, Melinda, but when the time came, you let me down. So I poisoned the bridal cup. It was necessary. And surprisingly easy. Who'd ever suspect the best man? No-one ever did, not even Walker himself." He looked at me suddenly, and he was smiling. "I was pretty sure my little problem had to be Melinda, but I needed you here to make certain. That's why I asked Walker to contact you, on my behalf. Because your talent to find things holds her in one place, one shape. All you have to do is hold her here, and my laser light will disrupt her, take her apart so thoroughly she'll never be able to put herself back together again. Do this for me, John, and I'll make you a partner in Prometheus Inc. You'll be wealthy and powerful beyond your wildest dreams."

"They were my friends, too," I said. "And there isn't enough money in the Nightside to turn me against a friend."

"Be my friend, John," said Melinda. She'd drifted very close now, and I could feel the cold of the grave radiating from her. "Be my friend and Quinn's, one last time. Find the source of Vincent's power. His secret source."

Vincent fired his laser at her. The light beam punched right through her shimmering form, but if it hurt her she didn't show it.

I called up my talent again, focussing my inner eye, my private eye from which nothing can be hidden, and immediately I knew where the secret was, and how to get to it. I turned to the steel door and punched in the correct entry codes. The heavy door swung slowly open. Vincent shouted something, but I wasn't listening. I walked through the opening, Melinda drifting after me, and there in the underground chamber Vincent had made specially for him, was the reason Vincent had been able to produce power so easily. It was Quinn, the Sunslinger.

He still looked a lot like he had in his wedding photo, but like Melinda, he had been through some changes. Quinn still wore his black leathers, though the steel and silver were dirty and corroded. His body was contained in a spirit bottle, a great glass chamber designed to contain the souls of the dead. Electricity cables penetrated the sides of the bottle, plugging into Quinn's eye sockets, his wedged-open mouth, and holes cut in his torso. Quinn, the Sunslinger, whose power had been to channel and direct energies from the sun, had been made into a battery. The spirit bottle trapped his soul with his dead body and made him controllable. The cables leached his power, and Vincent's machines turned it into electricity to feed the Nightside.

Ingenious. But then, the Mechanic had never been afraid to think big.

Melinda hovered beside the spirit bottle, staring at what had been done to her dead love with yearning eyes, unable to touch him for all her ghostly power. I ran my fingertips down the glass side of the spirit bottle, testing its strength.

"Get away from that, John," said Vincent.

I looked round to see Vincent stepping through the doorway, his laser gun trained on me. He laughed, a little shakily.

"Ordinary guns are no use against you, John. I know that. I know all about that clever trick you do with bullets. But this is a laser, and it will quite definitely kill you. It's a clever little device. Draws its power directly from Quinn. So you're going to do exactly what I tell you to do. You're going to use your talent to fix and hold Melinda in one place, one shape, while I kill her. Or I'll kill you. Slowly and very nastily."

"How will you stop Melinda without me?" I said.

"Oh, I'm sure I'll be able to think of something, now I know for sure it's Melinda. Maybe I'll build another spirit bottle, just for her."

"What happened?" I said, careful to keep my voice calm and my hands still. "You three were friends for years, closer than family. So what happened, Vincent? What turned you into a murderer?"

"They let me down," he said flatly. "When I needed them most, they weren't there for me. I dreamed up this power station, you see. A way at last to provide dependable electricity for the Nightside. A licence to print money. My big score, at last. And all I needed to make it work was Quinn. I was sure studying his powers under laboratory conditions would enable me to build something that would power the plant. But when I told him, he turned me down. Said his secrets were family secrets and not for sharing. After all the things I'd done for him! I talked to Melinda, tried to get her to persuade him, but she didn't want to know either. She and Quinn were planning a new life together, and there was no room in it for me.

"But I'd already sunk all my money into this project, and a hell of a lot more I'd borrowed from some really unpleasant people. It had never occurred to me that Quinn would turn me down. The project was already under way. It had to go on. So I killed Quinn and Melinda. It was their own fault, for putting their own selfish happiness ahead of my needs, my success. I would have made them partners. Made them rich. After they were dead, my financial associates retrieved

Quinn's body from his grave, leaving a duplicate behind, and brought him here. Where he ended up working for me anyway. My . . . silent partner, if you like."

Melinda looked at me, silently pleading. The spirit bottle was full of light, with no shadows she could use. I looked at the bottle thoughtfully. Vincent aimed the laser at my stomach.

"Don't even think it, John. If you break the bottle, that breaks the connection between Quinn and my machines, and that would shut down the whole plant. No more of my electricity for the Nightside. Power cuts everywhere. Thousands of people could die."

"Ah well," I said. "What did they ever do for me?"

It was the easiest thing in the world for my talent to find the entry point into the spirit bottle and nudge it open just a crack. That was all Quinn needed. His dead body convulsed and suddenly blazed with light. Brilliant sunlight, too bright for mortal eyes to look upon. Vincent and I both had to turn away, shielding our eyes with our arms. The spirit bottle exploded, unable to contain the released energies of the Sunslinger. Glass fragments showered down. I made myself turn back and look through dazzled eyes as Quinn strode out of the wreckage, pulling the cables out of his face and his body. They fell to twitch restlessly on the floor, like severed limbs.

The dead man looked upon the ghost, and they smiled at each other, together again for the first time since their wedding day. And Vincent stumbled forward with his laser gun. His eyes weren't really clear yet, and I wasn't entirely sure who he was trying to point the gun at, but I didn't feel like taking any chances. So I reached down, grabbed one of the twitching cables from the floor, and lunged forward to jam one end of the cable into Vincent's eye. It plunged into his eye socket, burrowing beyond, and Vincent screamed horribly as his own machines sucked the life energies out of him. He was dead before his twitching body hit the floor.

Melinda Dusk and Quinn—the Hanged Man's Beautiful Daughter and the Sunslinger—dead but no longer separated, were already gone, too wrapped up in each other to care about lesser needs like vengeance. Quinn's body lay still and empty on the floor beside that of his old friend Vincent. I looked at Quinn's body and thought about whether I should take it back to his family, for a proper burial. But I had no proof of what had happened here, and as long as the armed truce between the two families continued, it was better not to stir things up. After all, who would Vincent have gone to first for financial backing? Who did he know, who would still lend him money after all his failures, except for certain factions in the two families?

I walked out of the secret vault, leaving the dead past behind, and used my talent one last time to find the self-destruct mechanism for the power plant. I knew there had to be one. Vincent was always very jealous about guarding his secrets. I allowed myself enough time to get clear, then set the clock ticking. I told the security men outside to start running, and something in my voice and my gaze convinced them. I was three blocks away when the whole of Prometheus Inc. went up in one great controlled explosion. I kept walking and didn't look back.

Not exactly my most successful case. My client was dead, so I wasn't going to get paid. Walker was probably going to be pretty mad that the power plant was gone, and God alone knew how much damage its loss was going to cause the Nightside. But none of that mattered. Melinda Dusk and Quinn had been my friends. And no-one kills a friend of mine and gets away with it.

TWO

Between Cases

Everyone needs somewhere to go, when it all goes pear-shaped. A bolt-hole to shelter in, till the shitstorm passes. I usually end up in Strangefellows, the oldest bar in the world. A (fairly) discreet drinking establishment, tucked away in the back of beyond, at the end of an alley that isn't always there, Strangefellows is a good place to booze and brood and hide from any number of people, most of whom wouldn't be seen dead in such a dive. It was run with malice aforethought by one Alex Morrisey, who didn't allow any trouble in his bar, most especially from me.

I found a table in a corner, so I wouldn't have to watch my back, and indulged myself with a bottle of wormwood brandy. It tastes like a supermodel's tears and is so potent it can catch alight if someone at the next table strikes a match. I kept my head well down and looked about me surreptitiously. If anyone had noticed me come in, they were keeping their excitement well under control. Certainly no-one was rushing for the exit to tell on me. Perhaps word hadn't got around yet as to how royally I'd screwed up this time. There were any number of people who weren't going to be at all pleased with me for knocking out twelve per cent of the Nightside's electricity supply. Not least Walker, who'd got me the job in the first place. I faked a careless shrug. If they couldn't take a joke, they shouldn't hire me.

It was a quiet night at Strangefellows, for once. All the lights were out, and the whole place was illuminated by candles, hurricane lamps, and the occasional hand of glory. It gave the place a pleasant golden haze, like an old photo of better times. Alex explained when I got my drink that the power was down in various spots all over the Nightside, and I just nodded and grunted. Alex was severely pissed off by the inconvenience and loss of takings, but that was nothing new. Strangefellows's owner and bartender was a thin pale streak of misery who only wore black because no-one had come up with a darker colour yet. He wore a snazzy black beret to hide his bald patch and designer shades to tone down the perpetual glare with which he regarded the world.

He's a friend of mine. Sometimes.

Music was playing from a portable CD player, rising easily over the bare murmur of conversation from the few regulars nursing their drinks in the back booths. Most of the bar's usual crowd were probably out and

about in the Nightside, taking advantage of the blackouts to do unto others and run off with the takings. It
would be a busy time for the Nightside's fences, before
the lights went on again. Alex's pet vulture was
perched over the till, cackling to itself and giving the
evil eye to anyone who looked like getting too close.
The bar's muscular bouncers, Betty and Lucy Coltrane,
were occupying themselves with a flex-off at the end of
the bar, frowning seriously as muscles distended and
veins popped up all over their sculpted bodies. Pale
Michael was running a book as to which one would
pass out first.

And my teenage secretary, Cathy Barrett, was dancing wildly on a tabletop, to the music of Voice of the
Beehive's "Honey Lingers." Blonde, bubbly, and full of
more energy than she knew what to do with, Cathy ran
the business side of my life. I'd rescued her from a house
that tried to eat her, and she adopted me. I didn't get a
say in the matter. Dancing opposite her on the tabletop,
in a leather outfit, cape, mask, and six-inch stiletto heels,
was Ms. Fate, the Nightside's very own transvestite su-
perhero, a man who dressed up as a superheroine to fight
crime and avenge injustice. He was actually pretty good
at it, in her own way. Cathy and Ms. Fate danced their
hearts out, pounding their heels on the table to "Monsters and Angels," and I had to smile. They were the
brightest things in the whole bar.

I topped up my glass with the murky purple liquor
and drank to the memory of Melinda Dusk and Quinn.
It was good to know they were finally at rest, together,
their murders avenged. I don't have that many friends.
Either my enemies kill them, or I do. Morality can be a
shifting, treacherous thing in the Nightside, and both

love and loyalty have a way of getting drowned in the bigger issues. My few longtime friends have all tended to be dangerous as hell in their own right, and more than a little crazy. People like Razor Eddie and Shotgun Suzie . . . both of whom have tried to kill me in the past. I don't hold it against them. Much. It's a hard life in the Nightside, and a harder death, usually. I sipped my drink and listened to the music. I wasn't in any hurry. I had the rest of the bottle to get through.

I've never found it easy to mourn, though God knows I've had enough practice.

I looked around the bar, searching for something to distract myself with. A sailor had passed out at the main bar, and the tattoos on his back were quietly arguing matters philosophical over the low rumble of his snores. A mummy at the other end of the long wooden bar was drinking gin and tonics while performing necessary running repairs on his yellowed bandages. Roughly midway between the two, an amiable drunk in a blood-stained lab coat was endeavouring to explain the principles of retro-phrenology to a frankly disinterested Alex Morrisey.

"See, phrenology is this old Victorian science, which claimed you could determine the dominant traits of a man's personality by studying the bumps on his head. The size and position of these bumps indicated different personality traits. See? Now, *retro-phrenology* says, why not change a man's personality by hitting him on the head with a hammer, till you raise just the right bumps in the right places!"

"One of us needs a lot more drinks," said Alex. "That's starting to make sense."

Cathy suddenly slammed down into the chair opposite me, breathing harshly and radiating happy sweat. She flashed me a cheerful grin. She'd picked up a fresh flute of champagne from somewhere and drank from it thirstily. Cathy always drank "champers," and nearly always found a way to stick me with the bill.

"I love to dance!" she said cheerfully. "Sometimes I think the whole world should be put to music and choreographed!"

"This being the Nightside, someone somewhere is undoubtedly working on that very thing, right now," I said. "Where's your partner, the Dancing Queen?"

"Oh, he's nipped off to the loo, to freshen her make-up. You know, John, I could see you brooding from right across the room. Who died this time?"

"What makes you think someone died?"

"You only drink that wormwood muck when you've lost someone close to you. I wouldn't use that stuff to clean combs. I thought the Prometheus gig was a straightforward deal?"

"I really don't want to talk about it, Cathy."

"No, you'd rather sulk and be miserable and pollute the atmosphere for everyone else. If you're not careful, you'll end up like Alex."

Cathy could always make me smile. "There's no danger of that. I'm not in Alex's class. That man could brood for the Olympics, and pick up a bronze in self-pity while he was at it. He's why there's never been a Happy Hour in Strangefellows."

Cathy sighed, leaned forward, and gave me her best exasperated look. "Get another case going, John. You know you're really only happy when you're working. Not that that's much healthier, given the cases you specialise in. You need to get out more and meet people, preferably people who aren't trying to kill you. You know, I found this really great new dating site for professional singles on the Net the other day . . ."

I shuddered. "I've seen some of those. *Hi! I'm Trixi, and I've got diseases so virulent you can even catch them down a phone line! Just give me your credit card number, and I guarantee to make your eyes water in under thirty seconds!* No, Cathy! I'm quite happy with my solitary brooding. It builds character."

Cathy pouted, then shrugged. She never could stay unhappy for long. She finished off the last of her champagne, hiccuped happily, and looked hopefully round the bar for another dancing partner. I'd never admit it to her, but she was mostly right. My work was all I had to give my life meaning. But since my last successful case earned me a quarter of a million pounds, plus bonuses, I could afford to be more particular about what work I chose to take on. (I located the Unholy Grail for the Vatican, and faced down Heaven and Hell in the process. I'd *earned* that money.) Maybe I should start looking for a new case, if only to take the taste of Prometheus Inc. out of my mouth.

"I'm bored," Cathy announced, slapping both hands on the table to prove it. "Bored of sitting around your expensive new office with nothing to do. It's all very comfortable, I'm sure, and I love all the new equipment, but a growing girl can't spend all her life surfing dodgy porn sites on the Internet. Like you, I need to be doing. Earning my keep and smiting the ungodly where it hurts. There must be something in all the messages I've taken that appeals to you. What about the case of the missing shadows? Or the guy who lost his adolescence in a rigged card game?"

"Hold everything," I said sternly. "A disturbing thought has just occurred to me. Who's looking after things in my expensive new Nightside office, while you're out cavorting and carousing in dubious drinking establishments?"

"Ah," said Cathy, grinning. "I got a really good deal on some computers from the future. They practically run the whole business on their own, these days. They can even answer the phone and talk snotty to our creditors."

"Just how far up the line did these computers come from?" I said suspiciously. "I mean, are we talking Artificial Intelligence here? Are they going to want paying?"

"Relax! They're data junkies. The Nightside fascinates them. Why don't we ask them to find something that would interest you?"

"Cathy, I only took on the Prometheus case to keep you quiet . . ."

"No you didn't!" Cathy said hotly. "You took that on because you wanted Walker to owe you a favour."

I scowled and addressed myself to my drink. "Yes, well, that didn't actually work out as well as I'd hoped."

"Oh God," said Cathy. "Am I going to have start locking the doors and windows and hiding under the desk again, when he comes around?"

"I think it would be a better idea if we both stayed away from the office completely, just for a while."

"That bad?"

"Pretty much. Let Walker argue with the computers and see how far it gets him."

There was a sudden flare of brilliant light, and a man

fell out of nowhere into Strangefellows. He crashed to the floor just in front of the bar, his New Romantic silks in shreds and tatters. Static sparks discharged from every metal object in the bar, and the air was heavy with the stench of ozone—the usual accompanying signs of time travel. The newcomer groaned, sat up, and wiped at his bloody nose with the back of his hand. He'd clearly been through a hell of a fight recently, and just as clearly lost. I knew him, though if I met him in the street, I tried very hard not to. He was Tommy Oblivion, a fellow private investigator, though he specialised in cases of an existential nature. He lurched to his feet, leaned his back against the bar for support while he pulled his ragged silks around him, then saw me watching him. His battered face purpled with rage, and he stabbed a shaking finger at me.

"You! Taylor! This is all your fault! I'll have your balls for this!"

"I haven't seen you in months, Tommy," I said calmly.

"No, but you will! In the future! Only this time I'll be ready for you, and better prepared! I'll have guns! Big guns!"

He continued to spit abuse at me, but I couldn't be bothered. I looked at Alex, and he gestured at his two bouncers. Betty and Lucy hurried forward, glad of an excuse for a little action. Tommy made the mistake of threatening them, too, and the two girls briskly knocked him to the floor, kicked him somewhere painful, and then frog-marched him out of Strangefellows. Cathy gave me a hard look.

"What was that all about?"

"Beats the hell out of me," I said honestly. "Presumably I'll find out. In time."

"Excuse me," said a voice with a cultured French accent. "Have I the honour of addressing Mr. John Taylor?"

Cathy and I both looked round sharply. Standing right before us was a short, comfortably padded, middle-aged man in an expertly cut suit. He looked supremely elegant, not a hair out of place, and his smile was sophisticated charm itself. There was no way he could have entered the bar and approached my corner table without being seen, but there he was, large as life and twice as French. He nodded courteously to me, smiled at Cathy, and kissed her proffered hand. She gave him a dazzling smile in return. I decided not to like him, on general principles. I really don't like being sneaked up on. It's bad for my health. I gestured for the Frenchman to pull up a chair. He studied the empty chair solemnly for a moment, then produced a blindingly white handkerchief from an inner pocket and flicked the seat of the chair a few times before deigning to sit on it. I gave him my best intimidating glare, to remind him who was boss around here.

"I'm John Taylor," I growled. "You're a long way from home, *m'sieu*. What can I do for you?"

He nodded easily, entirely unimpressed. "I am Charles Chabron, for many years one of the most respected bankers in Paris. And I have come a very long way to meet with you, Mr. Taylor, and inquire whether I might hire your professional services."

"Who recommended me to you?" I said carefully.

He flashed his charming smile again. "An old friend of yours who does not wish to be identified."

He had me there. "I get a lot of that," I admitted. "What is it you want, Mr. Chabron?"

"Please, call me Charles. I am here because of my daughter. You may have heard of her. She is currently the new singing sensation of the Nightside. She calls herself Rossignol, though that is of course not her real name. Rossignol is merely French for nightingale. She first came to London, then the Nightside, some five years ago, determined to make for herself a career as a singer. And this last year she has been singing very successfully to packed houses in nightclubs all over the Nightside. I understand there's even talk of a recording contract with one of the major companies. Which is all well and good.

"However, since she took up with her new management, a Mr. and Mrs. Cavendish, she only sings at one nightclub, Caliban's Cavern, and she has . . . changed. She has broken off all contact with her old friends and family. She does not answer phone calls or letters, and her new management won't let anyone get near her. They say they do this at her explicit request and justify it in the name of protecting her from over-zealous fans of her new fame. But I am not so sure. Her mother is frantic with worry, convinced that the Cavendishes have poisoned our daughter's mind against her family, and that they are, perhaps, taking advantage of her. And so I have come here, to you, Mr. Taylor, in the hope that you can establish the truth of the matter."

I looked at Cathy. The music scene was her speciality. There wasn't a club in the Nightside she hadn't drunk, danced, and debauched in at one time or another. She was already nodding.

"Yeah, I know Rossignol. And the Caliban club, and

the Cavendishes. They run Cavendish Properties. They have a collective finger in practically every big deal in the Nightside. They were big in real estate, until the market crashed just recently, after the angel war. Lot of people lost a lot of money in that disaster. Mr. and Mrs. Cavendish moved sideways into entertainment, representing clubs, groups, people . . . nothing really mega yet, but they've quickly made themselves a power to be reckoned with. Other agents cross themselves when they see the Cavendishes coming."

"What sort of people are they?" I asked.

Cathy frowned. "If the Cavendishes have first names, no-one knows or uses them. They don't get out much, preferring to work through intermediaries. Not at all averse to playing hardball during negotiations, but then, nice people don't tend to last long in show business. There are rumours they're brother and sister, as well as husband and wife . . . Cavendish Properties is based on *old* money, going back centuries, but there's a lot of gossip going round that says the current owners are hungry for money and not too fussy about how they acquire it. There's also supposed to be a scandal about their last attempt at building Sylvia Sin into a singing sensation. But they spent a lot of money to cover it up. But there's always gossip in the Nightside. They could be on the level with Rossignol. I just hope her agent checked the small print in their contract carefully."

"She has no agent," said Chabron. "Cavendish Properties represents Rossignol. You can understand why I am so concerned."

I looked at him thoughtfully. There were things he wasn't telling me. I could tell.

"What brought your daughter all the way to London,

and the Nightside?" I said. "Paris has its own music scene, doesn't it?"

"Of course. But London is where you have to go to be a star. Everyone knows that." Chabron sighed. "Her mother and I never took her singing seriously. We wanted her to take up a more respectable occupation, something with a future and a pension plan. But all she ever cared about was singing. Perhaps we pressured her too much. I arranged an interview for her, with my bank. An entry-level position, but with good prospects. Instead, she ran away to London. And when I sent people to track her down, she disappeared into the Nightside. Now . . . she is in trouble, I am sure of it. One hears such things . . . I wish for you to find my daughter, Mr. Taylor, and satisfy yourself on my behalf that she is well and happy, and not being cheated out of anything that is rightfully hers. I am not asking you to drag her back home. Just to assure yourself that everything is as it should be. Tell her that her friends and her family are concerned for her. Tell her . . . that she doesn't have to talk to us if she doesn't want to, but we would be grateful for some form of communication, now and then. She is my only child, Mr. Taylor. I need to be sure she is happy and safe. You understand?"

"Of course," I said. "But I really don't see why you want me. Any number of people could handle this. I can put you onto a man called Walker, in the Authorities . . ."

"No," Chabron said sharply. "I want you."

"It doesn't seem like my kind of case."

"People are dying, Mr. Taylor! Dying, because of my daughter!" He took a moment to calm himself, before continuing. "It seems that my Rossignol sings only sad songs these days. And that she sings these sad songs so powerfully that members of her audience have been known to go home and commit suicide. Already there are so many dead that not even her management can keep it quiet. I want to know what has happened to my daughter, here in your Nightside, that such a thing is possible."

"All right," I said. "Perhaps it is my kind of case after all. But I have to warn you, I don't come cheap."

Chabron smiled, back on familiar ground. "Money is no problem to me, Mr. Taylor."

I smiled back at him. "The very best kind of client. My whole day just brightened up." I turned to Cathy. "Go back to the office and get your marvelous new computers working on some background research. I want to know everything there is to know about the Cavendishes, their company, and their current financial state. Who they own, and who they owe money to. Then see what you can find out about Rossignol, before she went to work for the Cavendishes. Where she sang, what kind of following she had, the usual. Mr. Chabron . . ."

I looked around, and he was gone. There was no sign of him anywhere, even though there was no way he could have made it to any of the exits in such a short time.

"Damn, that's creepy," said Cathy. "How does he *do* that?"

"There's more to our Mr. Chabron than meets the eye," I said. "But then, that's par for the course in the Nightside. See what can you can find out about him, too, while you're at it, Cathy."

She nodded quickly, blew me a kiss, and hurried

away. I got up and wandered over to the bar. I shoved the cork back into the bottle of wormwood brandy and handed it over to Alex. I didn't need it any more. He made it disappear under the bar and gave me a smug smile.

"I used to know Rossignol. Bit skinny for my tastes, but a hell of a set of pipes on her. I hired her a few years back to provide cabaret, to add some class to the place. It didn't work, but then this bar is a lost cause anyway. You couldn't drive it upmarket with a chair and a whip."

"Were you eavesdropping again, Alex?"

"Of course. I hear everything. It's my bar. Anyway, this Rossignol was pretty enough, with a good if untrained voice, and more importantly, she worked cheap. In those days she'd sing anywhere, for peanuts, for the experience. She had this need, this hunger, to sing. You could see it in her face, hear it in her voice. And it wasn't just your usual singer's ego. It was more like a mission with her. I wouldn't say she was anything special back then, but I always knew she'd go far. Talent isn't worth shit if you haven't got the determination to back it up, and she had that in spades."

"What kind of songs did she sing, back then?" I asked.

Alex frowned. "I'm pretty sure she only sang her own material. Happy, upbeat stuff, you know the sort of thing, sweet but forgettable. There were definitely no suicides when she sang here, though admittedly this is a tougher audience than most."

"So she was nothing like the deadly diva her father described?"

"Not in the least. But then, the Nightside can change

anyone, and usually not for the better." Alex paused and gave the bar top a polish it didn't need, so he wouldn't have to look me in the eye as he spoke. "Word is, Walker's looking for you, John. And he is not a happy bunny."

"Walker never is," I said, carefully casual. "But just in case he shows up here, looking for me, you haven't seen me, right?"

"Some things never change," said Alex. "Go on, get out of here, you're lowering the tone of the place."

I left Strangefellows and walked out into the night. One by one the neon signs were flickering on again, like road signs in Hell. I decided to take that as a good omen and kept walking.

THREE

Downtime in Uptown

If you're looking for the real nightlife in the Nightside, you have to go Uptown. That's where you'll find
the very best establishments, the sharpest pleasures,
the most seductive damnations. Every taste catered
for, satisfaction guaranteed or your soul back. They
play for keeps in Uptown, which is, of course, part of
the attraction. It was a long way from Strangefellows,
so I took my courage in both hands, stepped right up
to the very edge of the passing traffic, and hailed a
sedan chair.

The sedan chair was part of a chain I recognised, or
I wouldn't have got in it. The traffic that runs end-
lessly through the rain-slick streets of the Nightside
can be a peril to both body and soul. I settled myself

comfortably on the crimson padded leather seat, and the sedan chair moved confidently out into the flow. The tall wooden walls of the box were satisfyingly solid, and the narrow windows were filled with bulletproof glass. They were proof against a lot of other things, too. There was no-one carrying the chair, front or back. This particular firm was owned and run by a family of amiable poltergeists. They could move a lot faster than human bearers, and even better, they didn't bother the paying customers with unwanted conversation. Poltergeist muscle was also handy when it came to protecting their chairs from the other traffic on the roads. The Nightside is a strange attractor for all kinds of traffic, from past, present, and future, and a lot of it tended towards the predatory. There are taxis that run on deconsecrated altar wine, shining silver bullets that run on demons' tears and angels' urine, and things that only look like cars but are always hungry.

A pack of headless bikers tried to crowd the sedan chair with their choppers, but the operating poltergeist flipped them away like poker chips. The roaring traffic gave us a bit more room after that, and it wasn't long at all before we were cruising through Uptown. You could almost smell the excitement, above the blood, sweat, and tears. Nowhere does the neon blaze more brightly, neon noir and Technicolor temptation, the sleazy signs pulsing like an aroused heartbeat. You can bet the lights here never even dimmed during the recent power outages. Uptown would always have first call on whatever power was available. But even so, it's always that little bit darker here, in the world of three o'clock in the morning, where the pleasures of the night need never end, as long as your money holds out.

You can find the very best restaurants in Uptown, featuring dishes from cultures that haven't existed for centuries, using recipes that would be banned in saner places. There are even specialised restaurants, offering meals made entirely from the meats of extinct or imaginary animals. You haven't lived till you've tasted dodo drumsticks, roc egg omelettes, Kentucky-fried dragon, kraken sushi surprise, chimera of the day, or basilisk eyes (that last entirely at your own risk). You can find food to die for, in Uptown.

Bookshops contain works written in secret by famous authors, never intended to be published. Ghost-written books, by authors who died too soon. Volumes on spiritual pornography, and the art of tantric murder. Forbidden knowledge and forgotten lore, and guide-books for the hereafter. One shop window boasted a new edition of that infamous book *The King in Yellow*, whose perusal drove men mad, together with a special pair of rose-tinted spectacles to read it through.

People bustled through the streets, following the lure of the rainbow neon. Scents of delicious cooking pulled at the nose, and snatches of beguiling music spilled from briefly opened doors. Long lines waited patiently outside theatres and cabaret clubs, and crowded round newstands selling the latest edition of the *Night Times*. More furtive faces disappeared into weapons shops, or brothels, where for the right price you could sleep with famous women from fiction. (It wasn't the real thing, of course, but then it never is, in such places.) Uptown held every form of entertainment the mind could conceive, some of which would eat you alive if you weren't sharp enough.

And nightclubs, of every form and persuasion. Music and booze and company, all just a little hotter than the consumer could comfortably stand. Some of the clubs go way back. Whigs and Tories argue politics over cups of coffee, then sit down to wager on demon-baiting matches. Romans recline on couches, pigging out on twenty-course meals, in between trips to the vomitorium. Other clubs are as fresh as today and twice as tasty. You'd be surprised how many big stars started out singing for their supper in Uptown.

The streets became even more thickly crowded as the sedan chair carried me deep into the dark heart of Uptown. Flushed faces and bright eyes everywhere, high on life and eager to throw their money away on things they only thought they needed. In and among the fevered punters, the people who earned their living in the clubs and nightspots of Uptown rushed from one establishment to another, working the several jobs it took to pay their rent or quiet their souls. Singers and actors, conjurers and stand-up comedians, strippers and hostesses and specialist acts—all of them thriving on a regular diet of buzz, booze, and bennies. And walking their beats or standing on corners, watching it all go by, the ladies of the evening with their kohl-stained eyes and come-on mouths, the twilight daughters who never said no to anything that involved hard cash.

This still being the Nightside, there were always hidden traps for the unwary. Smoke-filled bars where lost week-ends could stretch out for years, and clubs where people couldn't stop dancing, even when their feet left bloody marks on the dance floor. Markets where you could sell any part of your body, mind, or soul. Or someone else's. Magic shops that offered wonderful items and objects of power, with absolutely no guarantee they'd perform as advertised, or even that the shop would still be there when you went back to complain.

There were homeless people, too, in shadowed doorways and the entrances of alleyways, wrapped in shabby coats or tattered blankets, with their grubby hands held out for spare change. Tramps and vagabonds, teenage runaways and people just down on their luck. Most passersby have the good sense to drop them the odd coin or a kind word. Karma isn't just a concept in the Nightside, and a surprising number of street people used to be Somebody once. It's always been easy to lose everything, in the Nightside. So it was wise to never piss these people off, because they might still have a spark of power left in them. And because it might just be you there, one day. The wheel turns, we all rise and fall, and nowhere does the wheel turn faster than in Uptown.

The sedan chair finally dropped me off right outside Caliban's Cavern. I checked the meter, added a generous tip, and dropped the money into the box provided. No-one ever cheats the poltergeists. They tend to take it personally and reduce your home to its original components while you're still in it. The chair moved off into the traffic again, and I studied the nightclub before me, taking my time. People flowed impatiently around me, but I ignored them, concentrating on the feel of the place. It was big, expensive, and clearly exclusive, the kind of place where you couldn't get in, never mind get a good table, unless your name was on someone's list. Caliban's Cavern wasn't for just anybody, and that, of course, was part of the attraction. Rossignol's name blazed above the door in Gothic neon script, giving the times of her three shows a night. A sign on the closed front door made it clear the club was currently in between shows and not open for business. Even the most upmarket clubs have to take time out to freshen the place up in between sets. A good time for someone like me to do a little sneaking around. But first, I wanted to make sure this wasn't a setup of some kind.

I have enemies who want me dead. I don't know who or why, but they've been sending agents to try and kill me ever since I was a child. It has something to do with my absent mother, who turned out not to be human. She disappeared shortly after my father discovered that, and he spent what little was left of his life drinking himself to death. I like to think I'm made of harder stuff. Sometimes I don't think about my missing mother for days on end.

I studied the crowd bustling around and past me, but didn't spot any familiar faces. And the sedan chair would have let me know if someone had tried to follow us. But the case could be nothing more than a way of bringing me here, so that I could be ambushed. It's happened before. The only way to be sure there were no hidden traps was to use my Sight, my special gift that lets me find anything, or anyone. And that was dangerous in itself. When I open up my third eye, my private eye, my mind burns very brightly in the endless night, and all kinds of people can see me and where I am. My enemies are always watching. But I needed to know, so I opened up my mind and Saw the larger world.

Even in the Nightside there are secret depths, hidden layers, above and below. I could See ghosts all around me, running through their routines like shimmering video loops, moments trapped in Time. Ley lines blazed so brightly even I couldn't look at them directly, criss-crossing in brilliant designs, plunging through people and buildings as though they weren't really there. In the passing crowds, dark and twisted things rode on people's backs—obsessions, hungers, and addictions. Some of them recognised me and bared needle teeth in defiant snarls to warn me off. Giants walked in giant steps, towering high above the tallest buildings. And flitting here and there, the Light People, forever bound on their unknowable missions, occasionally drawn to this person or that for no obvious reason, but never interfering.

But what really caught my third eye were the layers of magical defences surrounding Caliban's Cavern. Intersecting strands of hexes, curses, and anti-personnel runes covered every possible way in and out of the club, all of them positively radiating maleficent energies. This was heavy-duty, hard-core protection, way out of the range of even the most talented amateurs. Which meant someone had paid a pro a small fortune, just to protect an up-and-coming singing sensation. However, none of those defences were targeted specifically at me, which argued against this being a trap. I shut down my Sight and looked thoughtfully at the closed door before me. As long as I didn't use magic, the defences couldn't see me, so . . . I'd just have to think my way past them.

Luckily, most magical defences aren't very bright. They don't have to be. I grinned, stepped forward, and knocked firmly on the door. A staggeringly ugly face rose before me, forming itself out of the wood of the door. The varnish cracked loudly as the face scowled at me. Wooden lips parted, revealing large jagged wooden teeth.

"Forget it. Go away. Push off. The club is closed between acts. No personal appearances from the artistes, no autographs, and no, you don't get to hang around the stage door. If you want tickets, the booking office will be open in an hour. Come back then, or not at all. See if I care."

Its message over, the face began to subside back into the door again. I knocked again on the broad forehead, and the face blinked at me, surprised.

"You have to let me in," I said. "I'm John Taylor."

"Really? Congratulations. Now piss off and play with the traffic. We are very definitely closed, not open, and why are you still standing there?"

There's nothing easier to outmanoeuvre than a pushy simulacrum with a sense of its own self-importance. I gave the face my best condescending smile. "I'm John Taylor, here to speak with Rossignol. Open the door, or I'll do all kinds of horrible things to you. On purpose."

"Well, pardon me for existing, Mr. *I'm going to be Somebody someday.* I've got my orders. No-one gets in unless they're on the list, or they know the password, and it's more than my job's worth to make exceptions. Even if I felt like it. Which I don't."

"Walker sent me." That one was always worth a try.

People were even more scared of Walker than they were of me. With very good reason.

The face in the door sniffed loudly. "You got any proof of that?"

"Don't be silly. Since when have the Authorities ever bothered with warrants?"

"No proof, no entry. Off you go now. Hop like a bunny."

"And if I don't?"

Two large gnarled hands burst out of the wood, reaching for me. There was no way of dodging them, so I didn't try. Instead, I stepped forward inside their reach and jabbed one hand into the wooden face, firmly pressing one of my thumbs into one of its eyes. The face howled in outrage. I kept up the pressure, and the hands hesitated.

"Play nice," I said. "Lose the arms."

They snapped back into the wood and were gone. I took my thumb out of the eye, and the face pouted at me sullenly.

"Big bully! I'm going to tell on you! See if I don't!"

"Let me in," I said. "Or there will be . . . unpleasantness."

"You can't come in without saying the password!"

"Fine," I said. "What's the password?"

"You have to tell me."

"I just did."

"No you didn't!"

"Yes I did. Weren't you listening, door? What did I just say to you?"

"What?" said the face. "What?"

"What's the password?" I said sternly.

"Swordfish!"

"Correct! You can let me in now."

The door unlocked itself and swung open. The face had developed a distinct twitch and was muttering querulously to itself as the door closed behind me. The club lobby looked very plush, or at least, what little of it I could see beyond the great hulking ogre that was blocking my way. Eight feet tall and almost as wide, he wore an oversized dinner jacket and a bow tie. The ogre flexed his muscled arms menacingly and cracked his knuckles loudly. One look at the low forehead and lack of chin convinced me there was absolutely no point in trying to talk my way past this guardian. So I stepped smartly forward, holding his eyes with mine, and kicked him viciously in the unmentionables. The ogre whimpered once, his eyes rolled right back in their sockets, and he fell over sideways. He hit the lobby floor with a crash and stayed there, curled into a ball. The bigger they are, the easier some targets are to hit. I walked unchallenged past the ogre and all the way across the lobby to the swinging doors that led into the nightclub proper.

Most of the lights were turned down here, and the cavern was all gloom and shadows. Bare stone walls under a threateningly low stone ceiling, a waxed and polished floor, high-class tables and chairs, and a raised stage at the far end. The chairs were stacked on top of the tables at the moment, and there were multi-coloured streamers curled around them and scattered across the floor. The only oasis of light in the club was the bar, way over to the right, open now just for the club staff and the artistes. A dozen or so night-time souls clustered together at the bar, like bedraggled moths drawn to the light.

I stepped out across the open floor towards them. Nobody challenged me. They just assumed that if I'd got in, I was supposed to be there. I nodded politely to the cleaning staff, busy getting the place ready for the next shift—half a dozen monkeys in bellhop uniforms, hooting mournfully as they pushed their mops around, passing a single hand-rolled back and forth between them. Lots of monkeys doing menial work in the Nightside these days. Some still even have their wings.

At the bar, the ladies in their faded dressing gowns and wraps didn't even look up as I joined them. The smell of gin and world-weariness was heavy on the air. Come showtime, these women would be all dolled up in sparkly costumes, with fishnet tights and high heels and tall feathers bobbing over their heads, hair artificially teased, faces bright with gaudy make-up . . . but that was then, and this was now. In the artificial twilight of the empty club, the chorus line and backup singers and hostesses wore no make-up, had their hair up in curlers, and as often as not a ciggie protruding grimly from the corner of a hardened mouth. They looked like soldiers resting from an endless war.

The bartender was some kind of elf. I can never tell them apart. He looked at me suspiciously.

"Relax," I said. "I'm not from Immigration. Just a special investigator, hoping to spread a little bribe money around where it'll do the most good for everyone concerned."

The ladies gave me their full attention. Cold eyes,

hard mouths, ready to give away absolutely nothing without seeing cold cash up front. I sighed inwardly, pulled a wad of folding money out of an inner pocket, and snapped it down on the bar top. I kept my hand on top of it and raised an eyebrow. A short-haired platinum blonde leaned forward so that the front of her wrap fell open, allowing me a good look at her impressive cleavage, but I wasn't that easily distracted. Though it really *was* impressive . . .

"I'm here to see Rossignol," I said loudly, keeping my eyes well away from the platinum blonde. "Where can I find her?"

A redhead with her hair up in cheap plastic curlers snorted loudly. "Best of luck, darling. She won't even speak to me, and I'm her main backing vocalist. Snotty little madam, she is."

"Right," said the platinum blonde. "Too good to mix with the likes of us. Little Miss Superstar. Speak to Ian, that's him up there on the stage. He's her roadie."

She nodded towards the shadowy stage, where I could just make out a short sturdy man wrestling a drum kit into position. I nodded my thanks, took my hand off the wad of cash, and walked away from the bar, letting the ladies sort out the remuneration for themselves. There was the sound of scuffling and really bad language by the time I got to the stage. I knocked on the wood with one knuckle, to get the roadie's attention. He came out from the drum kit and nodded to me. He seemed quite cheerful, for a hunchback. He swayed slightly from side to side as he came forward to join me, and I pulled myself up onto the stage. Up close, he was only slightly stooped on his bowed legs, with massive arms. He wore a T-shirt bearing the legend *Do Lemmings Sing the Blues?*

"How do, mate. I'm Ian Auger, roadie to the stars, travelling musician, and good luck charm. My grandfather once smelled Queen Victoria. What can I do for you, squire?"

"I'm looking to speak with Rossignol," I said. "I'm . . ."

"Oh, I know who you are, sunshine. John bloody Taylor, his own bad and highly impressive self. Private eye and king-in-waiting, if you believe the gossip, which I mostly don't. You're here about the suicides, I suppose? Thought so. Word was bound to get out eventually. I warned them, I said they couldn't hope to keep a lid on it for long, but does anyone here ever listen to me? What do you think?" He grinned cheerfully and lit up a deadly little black cigar with a battered gold lighter. "So, John Taylor. You here to make trouble for my little girl?"

"No," I said carefully. Behind the cheerful conversation, Ian's blue eyes were as cold as ice, and he had the look of someone who had very straight forward ideas on how to deal with problems. And the ideas probably involved blunt instruments. "I'm just interested in what's happening here. Maybe I can find a solution. It's what I do."

"Yeah, I've heard of some of the things you do." He considered the matter for a long moment, then shrugged. "Look, mate, I've been with Ross a long time. I'm her roadie, I set up the equipment and do the sound checks, I play her music, I take care of all the shit work so she doesn't have to. I look after her, right? I do the work of three men, and I don't begrudge a moment of it, because she's worth it. I've roadied for all sorts in my time, but she's the real thing. She's going to be big, really big. I was her manager, originally. The first one to see what she had and what she could be. I took her here and there in the Nightside, got her started, but I always knew she'd leave me behind. It doesn't matter. A voice like hers comes along once in a lifetime. I just wanted to be part of her legend."

"I thought Rossignol was managed by the Cavendishes," I said.

He shrugged. "I always knew she'd move on. I couldn't open the doors for her that the Cavendishes could. They're big, they're *connected*. But . . ."

"Go on," I prompted him, when he paused a little too long. He scowled and took his cigar out of his mouth and looked at it so he wouldn't have to look at me.

"This should have been Ross's big break. Caliban's Cavern; biggest, tastiest nightspot in the whole of Uptown. Just the right place to be seen, to be heard, to be *noticed*. But it's all gone wrong. She's changed since she came here. All she ever sings now are sad songs, and she sings them so powerfully that people in the audience go home and kill themselves. Sometimes they don't make it all the way home. God knows how many there've been . . . The Cavendishes are doing their best to cover it up, at least until the recording contract's signed, but word's getting out. They do so love to gossip in the music biz."

"Doesn't it put people off coming to see her?" I said.

Ian almost laughed. "Nah . . . that's all part of the thrill, innit? Makes her even more glamourous, to a certain type of fan. This is the Nightside, after all, always looking for the next new sensation. And Russian roulette is so last week . . ."

"What are the Cavendishes doing to investigate the phenomenon?"

"Them? Naff all! They never even show their faces down here. Just send the bullyboys around, to keep an eye on things, and put the wind up any investigative journalists that might come sniffing around." He smiled briefly. "They don't much care for private eyes either, mate. You watch yourself."

I nodded, carefully unimpressed. "Where can I find Rossignol?"

"She's still my girl," said Ian. "Even if she doesn't have much time for me these days. Are you here to help her, or are you just interested in the bloody *phenomenon*?"

"I'm here to help," I said. "Stopping innocent people dying has got to be in everyone's best interests, hasn't it?"

"She's in her dressing room, round the back." He gave me directions, then looked away from me, his gaze brooding and strangely sad. "I wish we'd never come here, her and me. This wasn't what I wanted for her. If it was up to me, I'd say stuff the money and stuff the contract, something's *wrong* here. But she doesn't listen to me any more. Hardly ever leaves her dressing room. I only get to see her when I'm onstage playing for her to sing to."

"Where does she go when she isn't here?"

"She's always here," Ian said flatly. "Cavendishes arranged a room for her, upstairs. Very comfortable, all the luxuries, but it's still just a bloody room. I don't think Ross has left the club once since she got here. Doesn't have a private life, doesn't care about anything but the next show, the next performance. Not healthy, not for a growing girl like her, but then, there's nothing healthy about Ross's career, since she took up with the bloody Cavendishes."

I started to turn away, but Ian called me back.

"She's a good kid, but . . . don't expect too much from her, okay? She's not herself any more. I don't know who she is, these days."

I found Rossignol's dressing room easily enough. The two immaculate gentlemen guarding her door weren't everyday bodyguards. The Cavendishes had clearly spent some serious money on internal security. These bodyguards wore Armani suits, and each bore a tattooed ideogram above his left eyebrow that indicated they were the property of the Raging Dragon Clan. Which meant they were magicians, martial artists, and masters of murder. The kind of heavy-duty muscle who usually guarded emperors and messiahs-in-waiting. A sensible man would have turned smartly about and disappeared, at speed, but I just kept going. If I let myself get intimidated by anyone, I'd never get anything done. I came to a halt before them and smiled amiably.

"Hi. I'm John Taylor. I do hope there's not going to be any unpleasantness."

"We know who you are," said the one on the left.

"Private eye, con man, boaster, and braggert," said the one on the right.

"King-in-waiting, some say."

"A man of little magic and much bluff, say others."

"We are combat magicians, mystic warriors."

"And you are just a man, full of talk and tricks."

I stood my ground and said nothing, still smiling my friendly smile.

The bodyguard on the left looked at the one on the right. "I think it's time for our coffee break."

The one on the right looked at me. "Half an hour be enough?"

"Three-quarters," I said, just to show I could play hardball.

The two combat magicians bowed slightly to me and walked unhurriedly away. They just might have been able to take me, but they'd never know now. I've always been good at bluffing, but it helps that most people in the Nightside aren't too tightly wrapped, at the best of times. I knocked on the dressing room door, and when no-one answered, I let myself in.

Rossignol was sitting on a chair, facing her dressing room mirror, studying her reflection in the mirror. She didn't even look round as I shut the door behind me. Her face was calm, and quietly sad, lost in the depths of her own gaze. I leaned back against the closed door and looked her over carefully. She was a tiny little thing, only five feet tall, slender, gamine, dressed in a blank white T-shirt and washed-out blue jeans.

She had long, flat, jet-black hair, framing a pale pointed face that was almost ghostly in the sharp un-

forgiving light of the dressing room. She had high
cheekbones, a long nose, pale pink lips, and not a
trace of make-up. If she was thinking anything, it did-
n't show in her expression. Her hands were clasped
loosely together in her lap, as though she'd forgotten
they were there. I said her name aloud, and she turned
slowly to face me. I did wonder for a moment whether
she might have been drugged, given a little something
to keep her calm and manageable, but that thought
disappeared the moment I met her gaze. Her eyes
were large and a brown so dark they were almost
black, full of fire and passion. She smiled briefly at
me, just a faint twitching of her pale mouth.

"I don't get many visitors these days. I like it that
way. How did you get past the two guard dogs at my
door?"

"I'm John Taylor."

"Ah, that explains many things. You are perhaps
the only person in the Nightside with a more disturbing reputation than mine." She spoke English perfectly, with just enough of a French accent to make
her effortlessly charming. "So now, why would the infamous John Taylor be interested in a poor little nightclub singer like me?"

"I've been hired to look into your welfare. To make
sure you're all right and not being taken advantage
of."

"How nice. Who hired you? Not the Cavendishes,
I assume."

I gave her a brief smile of my own. "My client
wishes to remain confidential."

"And I do not get a say in the matter?"

"I'm afraid not."

"It is my life we are discussing, Mr. Taylor."

"Please. Call me John."

"As you wish. You may call me Ross. You still haven't answered my question, John. What makes you think I need your assistance? I assure you, I am perfectly safe and happy here."

"Then why the heavy muscle outside your door?"

Her mouth made a silent moue of distaste. "They keep the more obsessive fans at bay. The over-enthusiastic and the stalkers. Ah, my audience! They would fill every moment of my life, if they could. I need time to myself, to be myself."

"What about friends and family?"

"I have nothing to say to them." Ross folded her arms across her chest and gave me a hard, angry stare. "Where were they when I needed them? For years they didn't want to know me, never answered my letters or my pleas for but a little support, to keep me going until my career took off. But the moment I became just a little bit famous, and there was the scent of real money in the air, ah then, suddenly all my family and my so-called friends were all over me, looking for jobs and hand-outs and a chance to edge their way into the spotlight, too. To hell with them. To hell with them all. I have learned the hard way to trust no-one but myself."

"Not even your roadie, Ian?"

She smiled genuinely for the first time. "Ian, yes. Such a sweet boy. He believed in me, even during the bad times when I was no longer sure myself. There will always be a place for him with me, for as long as he wants it. But at the end of the day, I am the star, and I will decide what his place is." She shrugged briefly. "Not even the closest of friends can always climb the ladder at the same pace. Some will always be left behind."

I decided to change the subject. "I understand you live here, in the club?"

"Yes." She turned away from me and went back to looking at herself in the mirror. She was looking for something, but I didn't know what. Maybe she didn't either. "I feel safe here," she said slowly. "Protected. Sometimes it seems like the whole world wants a piece of me, and there's only so much to go round. It's not easy being a star, John. You can take lessons in music, and movement, and how to get the best out of a song, but there's no-one to teach you how to be a success, how to deal with suddenly being famous and in demand. Everybody wants something . . . The only ones I can trust any more are my management. Mr. and Mrs. Cavendish. They're only interested in the money I can make for them . . . and I can deal with that."

"There have been stories, of late," I said carefully. "About mysterious, unexplained suicides . . ."

She looked back at me, smiling sadly. "You of all people should know better than to believe in such gossip, John. It's all just publicity stories that got out of hand. Exaggerations, to put my name on everyone's lips. Everyone claims to have heard the story direct from a friend of a friend, but no-one can ever name anyone who actually died. The Nightside does so love to gossip, and it always prefers bad news to good. I'm just a singer who loves to sing . . . Talk to the Cavendishes, if you're seriously worried. I'm sure they will be able to reassure you. And now, if you will be so good as to excuse me, I need to prepare myself. I have a show to do soon."

And she went back to staring at her face in the mirror, her chin cupped in one hand, her eyes lost in her own thoughts. I let myself out, and she didn't even notice I was gone.

FOUR

Cavendish Properties

I made my way back to the club bar, the tune from "There's No Business Like Show Business" playing sardonically in the back of my head. My encounter with Rossignol hadn't been everything it might have been, but it had been . . . interesting. My first impressions of her were muddled, to say the least. She'd seemed sharp enough, particularly her tongue, but there was no denying there was something *wrong* about Rossignol. Some *missing* quality . . . as though some vital spark had been removed, or suppressed. All the lights were on, but the curtains were a little too tightly closed. It didn't seem to be drugs, but that still left magical controls and compulsions. Not to mention soul thieves, mindsnakes, and even possession. There's never any shortage of potential suspects in the Nightside. Though what major players like that would want with a mere up-and-coming singer like Rossignol . . . Ah hell, maybe she was just plain crazy. No shortage of crazies in the Nightside either. In the end, it all came down to her singing. I'd have to come back again, watch her perform, listen to what she did with her voice. See what it did to her audience. After taking certain sensible precautions, of course. Certain defences. There are any number of magical creatures, mostly female, whose singing can bring about horror and death. Sirens, undines, banshees, Bananarama tribute bands . . .

Back at the bar I used their phone to call my new Nightside office and see how Cathy was getting on with her research into the Cavendishes. The elf bartender didn't raise any objections. He saw me coming and retreated quickly to the other end of the bar, where he busied himself cleaning a glass that didn't need cleaning. The chorus in their wraps and dressing gowns now had a bottle of gin each and were growing definitely raucous, like faded birds of paradise with a really bad attitude. One of them had produced a copy of the magazine *Duelling Strap-ons*, and they were all making very unkind comments about the models in the photos. I looked deliberately in the opposite direction and pressed the phone hard against my ear.

I don't use a mobile phone in the Nightside any more. It makes it far too easy for anyone to find me. Besides, signals here have a tendency to go weird on you. You can end up connected to all kinds of really wrong numbers, talking to anyone or anything, from all kinds of dimensions, in the past, present, and future.

And sometimes in between calls, you can hear something whispering what sounds like really awful truths . . . I had my last mobile phone buried in deconsecrated ground and sowed the earth with salt, just to be sure.

My secretary answered the phone before the second ring, which suggested she'd been waiting for my call. "John, where the hell are you?"

"Oh, out and about," I said cautiously. "What's the matter? Problems?"

"You could say that. Walker's been by the office. In his own calm and quiet way he is really not happy with you, John. He started with threats, escalated to open menace, and demanded to know where you were. Jail was mentioned, along with excommunication, and something that I think involves boiling oil and a funnel. Luckily, I was honestly able to say I hadn't a clue where you were, at the moment. You don't pay me enough to lie to Walker. He once made a corpse sit up and answer his questions, you know."

"I know," I said. "I was there. Where's Walker now?"

"Also out and about, looking for you. He says he's got something with your name on it, and I'm pretty sure it's not a warrant. Did you really black out half the Nightside? Do you need backup? Do you want me to contact Suzie Shooter or Razor Eddie?"

"No thank you, Cathy. I'm quite capable of handling Walker on my own."

"In your dreams, boss."

"Tell me what you've found out about the Cavendishes. Anything useful? Anything tasty?"

"Not much, really," Cathy admitted reluctantly.

"There's very little direct information available about Mr. and Mrs. Cavendish. I couldn't even find out their first names. There's nothing at all on them in any of the usual databases. They believe very firmly in keeping themselves to themselves, and their business records are protected by firewalls that even my computers from the future couldn't crack. They're currently sulking, by the way, and comforting themselves by sending abusive e-mails to Bill Gates. I've been ringing round, tapping all my usual sources, but once I mention the Cavendishes, most of them clam up, too afraid to speak, even on a very secure line. Of course, this being the Nightside, you can always find someone willing to talk . . . It's up to you how much faith you want to put in people like that."

"Just give me what you've got, Cathy."

"Well . . . Current gossip says that given the kind of deals the Cavendishes have been making recently—sales of property, calling in debts, grabbing at every short-term deal that's going—it's entirely possible they have an urgent need for money. Liquid cash, not investment. There are suggestions that either a Big Deal went seriously wrong, and won't be paying off as hoped, or that they need the money to support a new Big Deal. Or both. There are definite indications that the Cavendishes have recently moved away from their usual conservative investments in favour of high-risk/high-yield options, but that could just be the market."

"When did they make the move into show business?"

"Ah," said Cathy. "They've spent the last couple of years establishing themselves as big-time agents, managers, and promoters of up-and-coming new talent. They've thrown around a lot of money, without much to show for it so far. And again there's gossip that something went seriously wrong with their earlier attempt to promote a new singing sensation at Caliban's Cavern. Sylvia Sin really looked like she was going places for a time. Her face was all over the covers of the music and lifestyle magazines last year, but she went missing very suddenly, and no-one's seen her since. Sylvia Sin has completely disappeared, which isn't an easy thing to do, in the Nightside."

"Give me the bottom line, Cathy."

"All right. Cavendish Properties is an important, respectable, and wide-ranging business, with most of its money still in property and shares. Their showbiz ventures are backed up by serious capital investment, but though they've got dozens of acts on their books, Rossignol is the only potential big breakout. There's a lot of money riding on her being a big success. They can't afford for her to be another Sylvia Sin."

"Interesting," I said. "Thanks, Cathy. I'll look by later, when I get a chance. If Walker should show up again . . ."

"I know, hide in the loo and pretend no-one's home."

"Got it in one," I said. "Now, tell me where to find the Cavendishes."

Clearly the next logical step was to go and brace the Cavendishes in their lair and ask a few impertinent questions, so I left Caliban's Cavern and went walking through the long night, heading through Uptown towards the Business Area. It wasn't a long walk, and the crowds thinned away appreciably as I left show behind and headed towards business. In the end, it was like crossing a line between tinsel and glamour, and stark reality. Bright and gaudy clubs and restaurants were replaced by sober, stern-faced buildings, and the clamour of the Nightside at play was replaced by the thoughtful quiet of the Nightside at work. The Business Area was right on the edge of Uptown, and as close to respectable as the Nightside got. All City Gents in smart suits, with briefcases and rolled umbrellas. But it still payed to be wary—in the Nightside, business people aren't always people. Beings from higher and lower dimensions were always setting up shop here, hoping to make their fortune, and the battles were no less vicious for being waged in boardrooms.

The Cavendishes' building was right where Cathy had said it would be—an old Victorian edifice, still defiantly old-fashioned in aspect, with no name or number anywhere. Either you had business there, and knew where to find it, or the Cavendishes didn't give a damn. They weren't supposed to be easy to find. The Cavendishes weren't just successful, they were exclusive, like their club. I stood some distance away from the front door and looked the place over thoughtfully. The Cavendishes had surrounded their own private little kingdom with a hell of a lot of magical protection, most of it so strong I didn't even need to raise my Sight to detect it. I could feel it, like insects crawling over my skin. There was a tension on the air, of some terrible unseen watching presence, of immediate and dreadful danger. The building was definitely protected by Something, either from Above or Below. The feelings weren't strong enough to scare off anyone who had proper business in the building, but it was more than enough to put the wind up casual visitors or even innocent passersby. And certainly enough to keep most visitors cautious, and maybe even honest.

There was nothing subtle about this building's defences. The Cavendishes wanted everyone to know they were protected.

I approached the front door confidently, as though I had every reason to be there, and pushed it open. Nothing happened. I strode into the lobby like I owned the place, trying hard to ignore the feeling that I had a target painted on my forehead. The lobby was large, plush, very comfortable. Pictures on the walls, fresh flowers in vases, business men sitting in upholstered chairs, reading the *Night Times* and waiting to be called. I headed for the reception desk, and a young man and a young woman moved immediately forward to intercept me. It seemed I was expected. The two combat magicians at the nightclub must have phoned home. I smiled at the man and the woman heading my way, started to say something clever, and stopped. There was no point. They were both Somnambulists. Dressed in basic black, their faces were pale and calm and empty, their eyes tight shut. They were both fast asleep. Somnambulists rent out their sleeping bodies for other people to use. Usually they're indentured servants, paying off debts. They have no say in what's done with their bodies, and any resulting damage is their problem. Their owners, or more properly their puppet masters, can do anything they want, indulge any appetite or fantasy, for as long as the contract lasts. Or until the body wears out. That's the deal.

The real problem, for people like me, is that Somnambulists can't be bluffed or fooled or distracted by clever words. Which meant I was in real trouble. So I just shrugged and smiled and nodded to them, and said, "Take me to your leader."

The man punched me in the head. He moved so quickly I didn't even see it coming. I fell to the floor, and the woman kicked me in the ribs. I tried to scramble away, but in a moment they were all over me, both of them kicking me so hard I could feel ribs cracking. They kept in close, leaving me no room to escape, so I curled into a ball, protecting my head as best I could. The attack had been so sudden and so brutal I couldn't get my thoughts together to try any of my usual defences. All I could do was take it, and promise myself revenge later.

The beating went on for a long, long time.

Occasionally I'd get a glimpse of the other people in the lobby, but none of them even looked my way. They knew better than to get involved. They had their deals with the Cavendishes and absolutely no intention of putting them at risk. And I knew better than to call for help. I curled up tight, my body shuddering with every blow, damned if I'd give my enemies the satisfaction of hearing me cry out. And then one boot connected solidly with my head, and everything went fuzzy for a while.

The next thing I knew I was in an elevator, going up. The Somnambulists were standing on either side of my slumped body, faces empty, eyes closed. I lay still, doing nothing that might attract their attention. I hurt everywhere I could feel, pain so bad it made me sick. My thoughts were slow and drifting. I flexed my fingers slowly, then my toes, and they all worked. Breathing hurt, which suggested cracked and maybe even broken ribs. My mouth was full of blood. I let it drool out one side and tested my teeth with my tongue. A few felt worryingly loose, but at least I hadn't lost any. I hoped I hadn't wet myself. I hate it when that happens. It had been a long time since I took a beating this bad. Probably piss blood for a week. I'd forgotten the first rule of the Nightside—it doesn't matter how bad you think you are, there's always someone nastier. Still, this visit wasn't a total loss. I'd come looking for evidence that the Cavendishes were guilty of something, and this would do just fine.

The elevator stopped with a jerk that rocked my body, and the pain almost made me cry out. The doors opened, and the Somnambulists bent down, picked me up and carried me out. I didn't try to fight them. Partly because I wasn't in any shape to, but mostly because I was pretty sure they were taking me where I wanted to go—to meet their masters, the Cavendishes. They carried me across an office and dropped me like a rubbish bag before the reception desk. The thick carpet absorbed some of the impact, but it still hurt like hell, and I went away for a few moments.

When I came back, the Somnambulists were gone. I turned my head slowly, cautiously, and saw the door to an inner office closing. I relaxed a little and slowly forced myself up onto my hands and knees. New pains flared up with every move, and I spat mouthfuls of thick and stringy blood onto the luxurious carpet. I ended up sitting awkwardly, favouring the ribs on my left side, leaning the other side carefully against the reception desk for support. Someone was going to pay for this.

I was hurt, shaken, sick, and dizzy, but I knew I had to get my wits back together before the Somnambulists returned, to drag me before the Cavendishes. They didn't want me dead, or at least, not yet. The beating had been to soften me up, before the interrogation. Well, bad luck for them. I don't do soft. I had to wonder what they thought I knew . . . I eased a handkerchief out of my pocket with a shaking hand and gently mopped the worst of the blood from my bruised and beaten face. One eye was already so swollen and puffy that I couldn't see out of it. The handkerchief was so much a mess when I'd finished that I just dropped it on the expensive carpet. Let someone else worry about it.

I peered up and over the reception desk, and saw one of those icily gorgeous secretaries who are de rigueur in all the better offices. The kind who would bite their own limbs off before letting you past without an appointment. She studiously ignored me. The phone rang, and she answered it in a cool and utterly business-like way, as though there wasn't a half-dead private eye bleeding all over her lousy carpet. It could have been just another day in any office, anywhere.

I turned around slowly, gritting my teeth against the shooting pains, and put my back against the desk. After I'd got my breath back from the exertion, I realised there were other people in the office apart from me. In fact, there was quite a crowd of them, filling all the chairs, sitting cross-legged on the carpet, and leaning against the walls. Young, slim, fashionable and Goths to a boy and a girl, they lounged bonelessly, flipping

through music and lifestyle magazines, chatting quietly
and comparing tattoos, and checking out their elaborate
make-up in hand mirrors. They all had the same uniform of black on black, pale faces and heavy dark eye
make-up. Skin like chalk, eyes like holes—Death's
clowns. Piercings and purple mouths and silver ankhs
on chains. A spindly girl curled up in a chair noticed me
watching and put aside her copy of *Bite Me* magazine
to consider me dispassionately.

"Damn, they really put a world of hurt on you. What
did you do to make them mad?"

"I was just being me," I said, trying hard to keep my
voice sounding light and effortless. "I have this effect
on a lot of people. What are you doing here?"

"Oh, we're all just hanging out. We run errands, sign
fan photos for the stars, do a bit of everything really, just
to help out. In return, we get to hang, hear all the latest
gossip first. And sometimes we even get to meet the stars,
when they show up here. Our favourite's Rossignol, of
course."

"Of course," I said.

"Oh, she is just the best! Sings like a dark angel,
love and death all wrapped up in one easy-on-the-eyes
package. She sings like she's been there, and it's all
going to end tomorrow . . . we all just adore Rossignol!"

"Yeah," said a skull-faced boy, in his best sepulchral
growl. "We all love Rossignol. We'd die for her."

"What makes her so special?" I asked. "Worth dying
for?"

They all looked at me like I was mad.

"She is just so *cool*, man!" a barely legal girl said finally, tossing her long black hair angrily, and I knew that was all the answer I was going to get.

"So," said one of the others. "Are you, you know, anyone?"

"I'm John Taylor," I said.

They all looked at me blankly and went back to their magazines and their conversations. If you weren't in the music biz, you weren't anyone. And none of them gave a damn about my condition or predicament. They wouldn't risk doing anything that might get them banned from the office and their chance to meet the stars. Fans. You have to love them.

The door to the inner office swung open, and the Somnambulists reappeared. They headed straight for me, and I tried not to wince. They picked me up with brutal efficiency and half carried, half dragged me into the inner office. They dumped me on the floor again, and it took me a moment to get my breath back. I heard the door close firmly shut behind me. I forced myself up onto my knees, and then two hands slapped down hard on my shoulders to keep me there. Two stern figures were standing before me, wearing matching frowns, but I deliberately looked away. The inner office was surprisingly old-fashioned, almost Victorian in its trappings—all heavy furniture and solid comforts. Hundreds of identical books lined the walls, looking as old and well used as the furniture. No flowers here. The room smelled close and heavy, like clothes that had been worn too long.

Finally, I looked at my hosts. The Cavendishes resembled long spindly scarecrows clad in undertakers' cast-offs. Even standing still, there was something awkward and ungainly about them, as though they might topple over if they lost concentration. Their clothes were City Gent, both the man and the woman—characterless, anonymous, timeless. Their faces were unhealthily pale, the skin unnaturally perfect, without flaw or blemish, with that tight, taut look that usually comes from too many face-lifts. I didn't think so, in their case. The Cavendishes' faces were unlined because they'd probably never experienced an honest emotion in their lives.

They both stepped forward suddenly, to stand right in front of me, and their movements were eerily synchronised. Mr. Cavendish had short dark hair, a pursed pale mouth, and a flat, almost emotionless glare, as though I was less an enemy than a problem that needed solving. Mrs. Cavendish had long dark hair, good bone structure, a mouth so thin there were hardly any lips to it, and exactly the same eyes.

They made me think of spiders, contemplating what their web had brought them.

"You have no business here," the man said suddenly, the words cold and clipped. "No business. Isn't that right, Mrs. Cavendish?"

"Indeed it is, Mr. Cavendish," said the woman, in a very nearly identical voice. "Up to no good, I'll be bound."

"Why do you interfere in our business, Mr. Taylor?" said the man.

"You must explain yourself," said the woman.

Their manner of speech was eerily identical, almost without inflection. Their gaze bored into mine, stern and unblinking. I tried a friendly smile, and a thin rill of blood spilled down my chin from a split lip.

"Tell me," I said. "Is it really true you're brother and sister as well as husband and wife?"

I braced myself for the beating, but it still hurt like hell. When the Somnambulists finally stopped, at some unseen signal, it was only their grip on my shoulders that kept me upright.

"We always use Somnambulists," said the man. "The very best kind of servants. Isn't that so, Mrs. Cavendish?"

"Indeed yes, Mr. Cavendish. No back talk, and no treacherous independence."

"Good help is so hard to find these days, Mrs. Cavendish. A sign of the times, I fear."

"As you have remarked before, Mr. Cavendish, and quite rightly." The woman and the man looked at me all the time they were speaking, never once even glancing at each other.

"We know of you, John Taylor," said the man. "We are not impressed, nor are we disposed to endure your famous insolence. We are the Cavendishes. We are Cavendish Properties. We are people of substance and of standing, and we will suffer no intrusions into our affairs."

"Quite right, Mr. Cavendish," said the woman. "You are nothing to us, Mr. Taylor. Normally, you would be utterly beneath our notice. You are only one little man, of dubious parentage. We are a corporation."

"The singer Rossignol is one of our Properties," said the man. "Mrs. Cavendish and I own her contract. Her career and life are ours to manage, and we always protect what's ours."

"Rossignol belongs to us," said the woman. "We

own everything and everyone on our books, and we never let go of anything that's ours."

"Except to make a substantial profit, Mrs. Cavendish."

"Right you are, Mr. Cavendish, and I thank you for reminding me. We don't like anyone taking an unhealthy interest in how we manage our affairs, Mr. Taylor. It is no-one's business but ours. Many would-be heroes have tried to meddle in our concerns, down the years. We are still here, and mostly they are not. A wise man would deduce a useful lesson from these facts."

"How are you planning to stop me?" I said, not quite as distinctly as I would have liked. My lower lip was swelling painfully. "These sleeping beauties can't follow me around all the time."

"On the whole, we deplore violence," said the man. "It's so . . . common. So we have others perform it for us, as necessary. If you annoy us again, if you so much as approach Rossignol again, you will be crippled. And if you choose not to heed that warning, you will be killed. In a sufficiently unpleasant manner to discourage any others who might presume to interfere in our business."

"Still," said the woman, "we are reasonable people, are we not, Mr. Cavendish?"

"Business people, Mrs. Cavendish, first and foremost."

"So, let us talk business, Mr. Taylor. How much do you require to work for us, and only us?"

"To become one of our people, Mr. Taylor."

"A valued part of Cavendish Properties, and thus entitled to enjoy our goodwill, remuneration, and protection."

"Not a chance in hell," I said. "I'm for hire, not for sale. And I already have a client."

The Somnambulists stirred on either side of me, and I flinched despite myself, expecting another beating. A sensible man would have played along, but I was too angry for that. They'd taken away my pride—all I had left was my defiance. The Cavendishes sighed in unison.

"You disappoint us, Mr. Taylor," said the woman. "I think we will let the proper Authorities deal with you, this time. We have already contacted Mr. Walker, to complain about your unwanted presence, and he was most interested to learn of your present location. It seems he is most anxious to catch up with you. He is on his way here now, in person, to express his displeasure with you and take you off our hands. Whatever can you have done, Mr. Taylor, to upset him so?"

"Sorry," I said. "I never kiss and tell."

The Somnambulists started to move again, and I reached into an inside pocket of my trench coat and grabbed one of the packets I kept there for emergencies, recognising it immediately by shape and texture. I pulled the packet out as the Somnambulists leaned over me, tore it open, and threw the pepper into their faces. The heavy dark powder hit them squarely in the nose and eyes, and they both breathed it in before they could stop themselves. And then they were both sneezing, loud, vicious sneezes that made their whole bodies convulse. Tears rolled out from under their closed eyes, and they fell back from me, sneezing so hard and so often they could hardly stay upright. And still the sneezing went on as the pepper did its unrelenting work.

Both Somnambulists bent forward from the waist, tears forcing themselves from their closed eyes, and in a moment they were both wide awake. The shock to their systems had been too much, the sheer strength of the involuntary physical reactions had been enough to overcome their enforced sleep. They were both wide awake, and hating every moment of it. They clutched at each other for support and looked around through watering eyes. I lurched to my feet and glared at them both.

"I'm John Taylor," I said, in my very best Voice of Doom. "And I am really upset with you."

The two awakened Somnambulists looked at me, looked at each other, in between sneezes, then turned and ran. They practically fought each other over who got to go through the door first. I grinned, despite my split and swollen lips. There are times when a carefully cultivated bad reputation can come in very handy. So can pepper, and salt. I always keep packets of both in my pockets. Salt is very good for dealing with zombies, for tracing protective circles and pentacles, and as a general purifier. Pepper has many practical uses, too. I carry other things in my pockets, some of them potentially quite viciously nasty, and right then I was in a mood to use every single one of them on the Cavendishes.

I'd like to say I waited till I'd learned all I could before I used the pepper. But the truth is, it had taken me until then to find the strength of will to use it.

I fixed the Cavendishes with a heavy glare. They stared back, apparently unmoved, and the man turned abruptly, picked up a silver bell from his desk, and rang it loudly.

A transport pentacle flared into life in one corner of his office, the pentacle's design shining suddenly in bright actinic lines as it activated, and in a moment there was someone else in the room with us. Someone I knew. He was dressed very formally, in a midnight blue tuxedo, a blindingly white shirt and bow tie, and a sweeping opera cloak, complete with scarlet lining. His carefully styled hair was jet-black, as was his neatly trimmed goatee. His eyes were an icy blue, and his mouth was set in a supercilious sneer. Anyone else would have been impressed, but I knew better.

"Hello, Billy," I said. "Like the outfit. How long have you been a waiter?"

"You look a mess, John," the newcomer said, stepping elegantly out of the transport pentacle, which flickered away into nothing behind him. He checked his cuffs were straight and looked me over disapprovingly. "Nasty. I always said that someday you'd run into trouble your rep couldn't get you out of. And don't call me Billy. I am Count Entropy."

"No you're not," I said. "You're the Jonah. Count Entropy was your father, and a far greater man than you. I remember you, Billy Lathem. We grew up together, and you were a useless little tit then, too. I thought you wanted to be an accountant?"

"I decided there was no money in it. Real money is to be made working for people like the Cavendishes. They keep me on a very handsome retainer, just for such occasions as this. And since my father is dead, I have inherited his title. I am Count Entropy. And I'm afraid I'm going to have to kill you now, John."

I sniffed. "Don't try and impress me, Billy Lathem. I've sneezed scarier-looking objects than you."

Why do bad things happen to good people? Because people like Billy Lathem profit from them. Essentially, he had the power to alter and control probabilities. The Jonah could see all the intertwining links of destiny, the patterns in the chaos, and reach out to choose the one-in-a-million chance for everything to go horribly wrong, and make that single possibility the dominant one. He caused bad luck and delighted in disasters. He destroyed lives and brought down in a moment what it had taken others a lifetime to build. When he was a kid, he did it for kicks—now he did it for money. He was the Jonah, and the misfortunes of others were his meat and drink.

"You're not fit to be Count Entropy," I said angrily. "Your father was a mover and a shaker, one of the Major Powers, revered and respected in the Nightside. He redirected the great energies of the universe."

"And what did it get him, in the end?" said Billy, just as angrily. "He made an enemy of Nicholas Hob, and the Serpent's Son killed him as casually as he would a fly. Forget the good name and the pats on the back. I want money. I want to be filthy, stinking rich. The title's mine now, and the Nightside will learn to fear it."

"Your father . . ."

"Is dead! I don't miss him. He was always disappointed in me."

"Well gosh," I said. "I wonder why."

"I'm Count Entropy!"

"No. You'll only ever be the Jonah, Billy. Bad luck to everyone, including yourself. You'll never be the man your father was, and you know it. Your dreams are too small. You're just the Bad Luck Kid, a small-time thug for hire."

He was breathing hard now, his face flushed, but he controlled himself with an effort and gave me his best disdainful sneer.

"You don't look like much right now, John. Those Somnambulists really did a job on you. You look like a passing breeze would blow you away. It shouldn't be too difficult to find a blood clot in your heart, or a burst blood vessel in your brain. Or maybe I'll start with your extremities and work inwards. There are so many nasty things I can do to you, John, so many bad possibilities."

I smiled back at him, showing him my bloody teeth. "Don't you mess with me, Billy Lathem. I'm in a really bad mood. How would you like me to use my gift, and find the one thing you're really afraid of? Maybe if I tried really hard . . . I could find what's left of your daddy . . ."

All the colour fell out of his face, and suddenly he looked like a child dressed up in an adult's clothes. Poor Billy. He really was very powerful, but I've been playing this game a lot longer than he has. And I have this reputation . . . I nodded to the Cavendishes, turned my back on them, and walked out of their office. And then I got the hell out of their building as fast as my battered body could manage.

No-one tried to stop me.

FIVE

The Singer, Not the Song

I must be getting old. I don't take beatings as well as I used to. By the time I got out of the Cavendishes' building, my legs were barely holding me up, and a cold sweat was breaking out all over my face. Every breath hurt like someone had stabbed me, and a rolling blackness was moving in and out at the edges of my vision. There was fresh blood in my mouth. Never a good sign. I still kept moving, forcing myself on through sheer effort of will. I needed to be sure I was far enough away from the Cavendishes that they couldn't send the building's defence spells after me. And even when I was sure, I kept going, though I was having to stamp my feet down hard to feel the pavement beneath me. I might look a sight, with my swollen face and blood-stained trench coat, but I couldn't afford to appear weak and vulnerable. Not in the Nightside. There are always vultures hovering, ready to drop on anything that looked like prey. So, stare straight ahead and walk like you've got a purpose. I caught a glimpse of myself, reflected in a window, and winced. I looked almost as bad as I felt. I had to get off the streets.

I needed healing and general repairs, and time out to get my strength back. But I was a long way from home, and I couldn't go to any of my usual haunts. Walker would have his people staking them all out by now. Even the ones he wasn't supposed to know about. And if I called any of my friends or allies, you could bet Walker would have someone listening in. The man was nothing if not thorough.

Well, when you can't go to a friend, go to an enemy.

I dragged my battered, aching body down the street, glaring at everyone to keep them from bumping into me, and finally reached a public phone booth. I hauled myself inside and leaned heavily against the side wall. It felt so good to be able to rest for a moment that I briefly forgot why I'd come in there, but I made myself pick up the phone. The dial tone was loud and reassuring. There tends to be very little vandalism of public phone booths in the Nightside. The booths defend themselves, and have been known to eat people who venture inside for reasons other than making a call.

I didn't know Pew's current number. He's always on the move. But he always makes sure to leave cards in phone booths so that people can find him in an emergency. I peered blearily at the familiar card (bright white with an embossed bloodred crucifix) and stabbed out the numbers with an unsteady hand. I was pretty much blind in one eye by then, and my hands felt worryingly numb. I relaxed a little as I heard the number ringing. I studied the other cards plastered across the glass wall in front of me. The usual mixture—charms and potions and spells, love goddesses available by the hour, transformations and inversions, and how to do horrible things to a goat for fun and profit.

Someone picked up the phone at the other end and said, "This had better be important."

"Hello, Pew," I said, trying hard to sound natural through my puffed-up mouth. "It's John Taylor."

"What the hell are you doing, calling me?"

"I'm hurt. I need help."

"Things must really be bad if I'm your best bet. Why me, Taylor?"

"Because you're always saying you're God's servant. You're supposed to help people in trouble."

"People. Not abominations like you! None of us in the Nightside will be safe until you're dead and buried in unconsecrated ground. Give me one good reason why I should put myself out for you, Taylor."

"Well, if charity won't do it, Pew, how about this? In my current weakened state, I am vulnerable to all kinds of attack, including possession. You really want to face something from the Pit in my body, with my gift?"

"That's a low blow, damn you," said Pew. I could practically hear him thinking it over. "All right, I'll send you a door. If only because I'll never really be sure you're dead unless I've finished you off myself."

The phone went dead, and I put it down. There's no-one closer, outside of family and friends, than an old enemy.

I turned around, slowly and painfully, pushed the booth door open and looked outside. A door was standing right in front of me, in the middle of the pavement. Just a door, standing alone, old and battered with the paint peeling off in long strips, and a rough gap showing bare wood where the number had once been. Probably stolen. Pew lived by choice in the rougher neighbourhoods, where he felt his preaching was most needed. I left the phone booth and headed for the door with the last of my strength. Luckily everyone else was giving it plenty of room, probably because it was so obviously downmarket as to be beneath their notice. I hit the door with my shoulder, and it swung open before me, revealing only darkness. I lurched forward, and immediately I was in Pew's parlour. The door slammed shut behind me.

I headed for the bare table in front of me and leaned gratefully on it as I got my breath back. After a while, I looked around me. There was no sign of Pew, but his parlour seemed very simple and neat. One table, bare wood, unpolished. Two chairs, bare wood, straight-backed. Scuffed lino on the floor, damp-stained wallpaper, and one window smeared over with soap to stop people looking in. The window provided the only illumination. Pew took his vows of poverty and simplicity very seriously. One wall was covered with shelves, holding his various stock in trade. Just useful little items, available for a very reasonable price, to help keep you alive in a dangerous place.

The door at the far end of the parlour slammed open, and Pew stood there, his great head tilted in my general direction. Pew—rogue vicar, Christian terrorist, God's holy warrior.

"Do no harm here, abomination! This is the Lord's place! I bind you in his word, to bring no evil here!"

"Relax, Pew," I said. "I'm on my own. And I'm so weak right now, I couldn't beat up a kitten. Truce?"

Pew sniffed loudly. "Truce, hellspawn."

"Great. Now do you mind if I sit down? I'm dripping blood all over your floor."

"Sit, sit! And try to keep it off the table. I have to eat off that."

I sat down heavily and let out a loud, wounded sigh. Pew shuffled forward, his white cane probing ahead of him. He wore a simple vicar's outfit under a shabby and much-mended grey cloak. His dog collar was pristine white, and the grey blindfold covering his dead eyes was equally immaculate. He had a large head with a noble brow, a lion's mane of grey hair, a determined jaw, and a mouth that looked like it never did anything so frivolous as smile. His shoulders were broad, though he always looked like he was several meals short. He found the other chair and arranged himself comfortably at the opposite end of the table. He leaned his cane against the table leg so he could find it easily, and sniffed loudly.

"I can smell your pain, boy. How badly are you injured?"

"Feels pretty bad," I said. My voice sounded tired, even to me. "I'm hoping it's mostly superficial, but my ribs are holding out for a second opinion, and my head keeps going fuzzy round the edges. I took a real beating, Pew, and I'm not as young as I once was."

"Few of us are, boy." Pew got to his feet and moved unerringly towards the shelves that held his stock. Pew might be blind, but he didn't let it slow him down. He pottered back and forth along the wall, running his hands over the various objects, searching for something. I just hoped it wasn't a knife. Or a scalpel. I could hear him muttering under his breath.

"Wolfsbane, crows' feet, holy water, mandrake root, silver knives, silver bullets, wooden stakes . . . could have sworn I still had some garlic . . . dowsing rods, pickled penis, dowsing rod made from a pickled penis, miller medallions . . . Ah!"

Pew turned back to me, triumphantly holding up a small bottle of pale blue liquid. And then he stopped, his mouth twisted, and his other hand fell to the rosary of human fingerbones hanging from his belt. "How has it come to this? You, alone and helpless in my home, in my power . . . I should kill you, damnation's child. Bane of all the chosen . . ."

"I didn't get to choose my parents," I said. "And everyone said my father was a good man, in his day."

"Oh, he was," Pew said unexpectedly. "Never worked with him myself, but I've heard the stories."

"Did you ever meet my mother?"

"No," said Pew. "But I have seen the auguries taken shortly after your birth. I wasn't always blind, boy. I gave up my eyes in return for knowledge, and much good it's done me. You will be the death of us all, John. But my foolish conscience won't let me kill you

in cold blood. Not when you come of your own free
will, begging my help. It wouldn't be . . . honourable."

He shook his great head slowly, came forward, and
stopped just short of the table. He placed the phial of
blue liquid on the table before me. I considered it, as
he shuffled back to his chair. There was no identifying
label on the phial, nothing to tell whether it was a cure
or a poison or something else entirely. Pew collected
all kinds of things on his travels.

"Hard times are coming," he said suddenly, as he
sat down again. "The Nightside is very old, but it is not
forever."

"You've been saying that for years, Pew."

"And it's still true! I know things. I See more without my eyes than I ever did with them. But the further
ahead I look, the more unclear things become. By saving you here today, I could be damning every other
soul in the Nightside."

"No-one's that important," I said. "And especially
not me. What's in the phial, Pew?"

He snorted. "Something that will taste quite appalling, but should heal all your injuries. Knock it
back in one, and you can have a nice sweetie afterwards. But magic has its price, John, it always does.
Drink that, and you'll sleep for twenty-four hours. And
when you wake up, all your injuries will be gone, but
you'll be a month older. The price you pay for such ac-
celerated healing will be a life one month shorter than
it would otherwise have been. Are you ready to give
that up, just to get well in a hurry?"

"I have to," I said. "I'm in the middle of a case, and
I think someone needs my help now, rather than later.
And who knows, maybe I'll find a way to get the lost

month back again. Stranger things have happened, in the Nightside." I paused and looked at Pew. "You didn't have to help me. Thank you."

"Having a conscience can be a real bastard sometimes," said Pew solemnly.

I unscrewed the rusted metal cap on the phial and sniffed the thick blue liquid within. It smelled of violets, a sweet smell to cover something fouler. I tossed down the oily liquid in one and just had time to react to the truly awful taste before everything went black. I woke up lying on my back on the table. My first feeling was relief. Although I'd tried hard to sound confident, there was a real chance Pew might have decided to finish me off while he had the chance. He'd tried often enough in the past. I sat up slowly. I felt stiff, but there was no pain anywhere. Pew had taken off my trench coat and folded it up to make a pillow for my head. I swung my legs down over the side of the table and stretched slowly. I felt good. I felt fine. No pain, no fever, and even the taste of blood was gone from my mouth. I put my hand to my face and was startled to encounter a beard. A month of my life had flown by while I slept . . . I got to my feet, went over to the wall shelves, and scrabbled among Pew's stock until I came up with a hand mirror. My reflection was a surprise, if not a shock. I had a heavy ragged beard, already showing touches of grey, and my hair was long and straggling. I looked . . . wild, uncivilised, intimidating. I didn't like the new look. I didn't like to think I could look like that. Like someone Pew would have a right to hunt down and kill.

"Vanity, vanity," said Pew, entering the room. "I

knew that would be the first thing you'd do. Put the mirror back. They're very expensive."

I held on to it. "I look a mess!"

"You just be grateful I remembered to dust you once in a while."

"Have you got a razor, Pew? This beard has to go. It's got grey in it. It makes me look my age, and I can't have that."

Pew grinned nastily. "I have a straight razor. Want me to shave you?"

"I don't think so," I said. "I don't trust anyone that close to my throat with a sharp blade."

He chuckled and handed me a pearl-handled straight razor. One dry shave later, with the help of the hand mirror, and I looked like myself again. It wasn't a very good or even a very close shave, but I got tired of nicking myself. I handed back the razor, then did a few stretches and knee bends. I felt fit to take on the world again. Pew sat on his chair like a statue, ignoring me.

"Once you leave here," he said suddenly, "you're fair game again."

"Of course, Pew. You wouldn't want people to think you were getting soft."

"I will kill you one day, boy. The mark of the beast is upon your brow. I can See it."

"You know," I said thoughtfully, changing the subect, "I could use one last piece of help . . ."

"God save us all, haven't I done enough? Out, out, before you ruin my reputation completely!"

"I need a disguise," I said firmly, not moving. "I have to get back on my case, and I can't afford to be recognised. Come on, you must have something simple and temporary you can let me have . . ."

Pew sniffed resignedly. "Let this be a lesson to me. Never help the stranger upon his way, because he'll only take advantage, the bastard. Where is it you have to go next?"

"A nightclub called Caliban's Cavern."

"I know it. A den of iniquity, and the bar prices are an outrage. I'd make you a Goth. There are so many of the grubby little heathens around that place, one more shouldn't be noticed. I'll put a seeming on you, a simple overlay illusion. It won't last more than a couple of hours, and it certainly won't fool anyone with the Sight . . ." He was pottering along the shelves again, picking things up and putting them down until finally he came up with an Australian pointing bone. He jabbed it twice in my direction, said something short and aboriginal, and put the bone back on the shelf again.

"Is that it?" I said.

Pew shrugged. "Well, you can have all the chanting and gesturing if you want, but I usually save that for the paying customers. It's really nothing more than window dressing. When you get right down to it, magic's never anything more than power and intent, no matter what the source. Look in the mirror."

I did so, and again someone else looked back at me. My face was entirely hidden under a series of swirling black tattoos, thick interlocking lines that made up a series of designs of ancient Maori origin. Along with the shaggy hair, the new look made me completely unrecognisable.

"You'll need another coat, too," said Pew. "Your

trench coat's a mess." He held up a battered black leather jacket with *God Give Me Strength* spelled out on the back with steel studs. "You can have this instead."

I tried on the jacket. It was a bit on the large side, but where I was going they wouldn't care. I made my good-byes to Pew, and the parlour door opened before me, revealing a familiar blackness. I walked into the dark, and immediately I was back in Uptown again, only a few minutes' walk from Caliban's Cavern. I heard the door close firmly behind me and knew it would be gone before I could turn to look. I smiled. Pew probably thought he'd put one over on me, by keeping my trench coat. A personal possession like that, liberally stained with my own blood, would make a marvelous targeting device for all kinds of magic. Certainly Pew could use it to send all kinds of nastiness my way. Which was why I'd taken out a little insurance long ago, in the form of a built-in destructive spell for the trench coat. Once I was more than an agreed distance away, the coat would automatically go up in flames. As Pew should be finding out, right about now.

Of course, I'd been careful to transfer all my useful items from the coat to my nice new jacket before I left.

Pew was good, but I was better.

By the time I got back to Caliban's Cavern, the queue was already forming for Rossignol's next set. I'd never seen so many Goths in one place. All dark clothes and brooding faces, like a gathering of small thunderclouds. They were all talking nineteen to the dozen, filling the night with a clamour of anticipation and impatience. Every now and again someone would start chanting Rossignol's name, and a dozen others would take it up until it died away naturally.

Ticket touts swaggered up and down beside the queue, fighting each other to be the first to target latecomers, offering scalped tickets at outrageous prices. There was no shortage of takers. The growing crowd wasn't just Goths. There were a number of celebrities, complete with their own entourages and hangers-on. You could always recognise celebrities from the way their heads swivelled restlessly back and forth, on the lookout for photographers. After all, what was the point of being somewhere fashionable if you weren't seen being there?

The queue stretched all the way down the block, but I didn't let that bother me. I just walked to the very front and took up a position there like I had every right to be there. Nobody bothered me. You'd be amazed what you can get away with if you just exude confidence and glare ferociously at anyone who even looks like questioning your presence. One of the ticket touts was rude enough to make sneering comments about my tattoos, though, so I deliberately bumped into him and pickpocketed one of his best tickets. I like to think of myself sometimes as a karma mechanic.

Caliban's Cavern finally opened its doors, and the queue surged forward. The Cavendishes had hired a major security franchise, Hell's Neanderthals, to man the door and police the crowd, but even they were having trouble handling the pressure of so many determined Rossignol fans. They pressed constantly forward, shouting and jostling, and the security Nean-

derthals quickly realised that this was the kind of
crowd that could turn into an angry mob if its progress
was thwarted. They were there to see Rossignol, and
no-one was going to get in their way. So, the Hell's
Neanderthals settled for grabbing tickets and waving
people through. I would have given them strict orders
to frisk everyone for weapons and the like, but it was
clear any attempt to slow the fans down now would
have risked provoking a riot. The fans were close to
their goal, their heroine, and they were hungry.

Inside the club, all the tables and chairs had been
taken out to make one great open space before the
raised stage at the far end of the room. The crowd
poured into it, gabbling excitedly, and quickly filled
all the space available, packing the club from wall to
wall. I was swept along and finally ended up right in
front of the stage, with elbows digging into my sides,
and someone's hot breath panting excitedly on the
back of my neck. The club was already overpoweringly hot and sweaty, and I looked longingly across at
the bar, with its extra staff, but it would have taken me
ages to fight my way through the tightly packed
crowd. No-one else seemed interested in the bar. All
the crowd cared about was Rossignol. Their diva of the
dark.

There were far too many people in the club, packed
in like cattle in their stalls. It didn't surprise me. The
Cavendishes hadn't struck me as the type to care about
things like safety regulations and keeping fire exits
clear. Not when there was serious money to be made.

Set off by a single bright spotlight, a huge stylised
black bird (presumably someone's idea of a nightingale) covered most of the wall behind the stage. It

looked threatening, wild, ominous. Looking around, I could see the design everywhere on the fans, on T-shirts, jackets, tattoos, and silver totems hanging on silver chains. I could also see the celebrities jammed in the crowd like everyone else, their hangers-on struggling to form protective circles around them. There were no real movers or shakers, but I could see famous faces here and there. Sebastian Stargrave, the Fractured Protagonist; Deliverance Wilde, fashion consultant to the Faerie; and Sandra Chance, the Consulting Necromancer. Also very much in evidence were the supergroup Nazgul, currently on a comeback tour of the Nightside with their new vocalist. They looked just as freaked and excited as everyone else.

And yet, for all the excitement and passion in the air, the overall mood felt decidedly unhealthy. It was the wrong kind of anticipation, like the hunger of animals waiting for feeding time. The hot and sweaty air had the unwholesome feel of a crowd gathered at a car wreck, waiting for the injured to be brought out. These people weren't just here to hear someone sing—this was a gathering throbbing with erotic Thanatos. The mood was magic. Dark, reverent magic, from all the wrong places of the heart.

The crowd was actually quietening down, the chanting dying out, as the anticipation mounted. Even I wasn't immune to it. Something was going to happen, and we could all feel it. Something big, something far out of the ordinary, and we all wanted it. We needed it. And whether what was coming would be good or bad didn't matter a damn. We were a congregation, celebrating our goddess. The crowd fell utterly silent, all our eyes fixed on the stage, empty save for the waiting instruments and microphone stands. Waiting, waiting, and now we were all breathing in unison, like one great hungry creature, like lemmings drawn to a cliff edge by something they couldn't name.

Rossignol's band came running onto the stage, smiling and waving, and the crowd went wild, waving and cheering and stamping their feet. The band took up the instruments waiting for them and started playing. No introductions, no warm-up, just straight in. Ian Auger, the cheerful hunchbacked roadie, played the drums. And the bass and the piano. There were three of him. I felt he might have mentioned it earlier. Next a quartet of backing singers came bounding onstage, wearing old-fashioned can-can outfits, with teased high hairstyles, beautiful and glamorous, with bright red lips and flashing eyes. They joined right in, belting out perfect harmonies to complement the music, stamping their feet and flashing their frills, singing up a storm. And then Rossignol came on, and the massed baying of the crowd briefly drowned out the music. She wore a chic little black number, with long black evening gloves that made her pale skin look even more funereal. Her mouth was dark, and so were her eyes, so that she seemed like some old black-and-white photograph. Her feet were bare, the toenails painted midnight black.

She grabbed hold of the mike stand at the front of the stage with both hands and clung to it like it was the only thing holding her up. As the show progressed, she rarely let go of it, except to light a new cigarette. She stood where she was, her mouth pressed close to the mike like a lover, swaying from side to side. She had a cigarette in one corner of her dark mouth when she came on, and she chain-smoked in between and sometimes during her songs.

The songs she sang were all her own material; "Blessed Losers," "All the Pretty People," and "Black Roses." They had good strong tunes, played well and sung with professional class, but none of that mattered. It was her voice, her glorious suffering voice that cut at the audience like a knife. She sang of lost loves and last chances, of small lives in small rooms, of dreams betrayed and corrupted, and she sang it all with utter conviction, singing like she'd been there, like she'd known all the pain there ever was, all the darknesses of the human heart, of hope valued all the more because she knew it wasn't real, that it wouldn't help; and all the loss and heartbreak there ever was filled her voice and gave it dominion over all who heard it.

There were tears on many faces, including my own. Rossignol had got to me, too. I'd never heard, never felt, anything like her songs, her voice. In the Nightside it's always three o'clock in the morning, the long dark hour of the soul—but only Rossignol could put it into words.

And yet, despite all I was feeling, or was being made to feel, I never entirely lost control. Perhaps because I'm more used than most to the dark, or simply because I had a job to do. I tore my eyes away from Rossignol, reached inside my jacket pocket, and pulled out a miller medallion. It was designed to glow brightly in the presence of magical influence, but when I held it up to face Rossignol, there wasn't even a glimmer of a glow. So Rossignol hadn't been enchanted or possessed or even magically enhanced.

Whatever she was doing, it came straight from her, and from her voice.

The audience was utterly engrossed, still and rapt and silent, drinking their diva in with eyes and ears, immersing themselves in emotions so sharp and melancholy and compelling that they were helpless to do anything but stand there and soak it up. It was all they could do to come out of it to applaud her in between songs. The three Ian Augers and the quartet of backing singers were looking tired and drawn, faces wet with sweat as they struggled to keep up with Rossignol, but the crowd only had eyes for her. She hung on to her microphone stand as though it was a lifeline, smoking one cigarette after another, blasting out one song after another, as though it was all she lived to do.

And then, as she paused at the end of one song to light up another cigarette, a man not far from me pressed right up against the edge of the stage, a man who'd been staring adoringly at Rossignol from the moment she first appeared, smiled at her with tears still wet on his cheeks and drew a gun. I could see it happening, but I was too far away to stop it. All I could do was watch as the man put the gun to his head and blew his brains out. All over Rossignol's bare feet.

At the sound of the gun, the Ian Augers looked up sharply from their instruments. The backing singers huddled together, eyes and mouths stretched wide. Rossignol stared blankly down at the dead man. He was still standing there, because the press of the crowd wouldn't allow him to fall, even though half his head was missing. And in the echoing silence, the crowd slowly came back to themselves. As though they'd been shocked awake from a deep dark dream where they'd all been drifting towards . . . something. I knew, because I'd been feeling it too. Part of me recognised it.

Then the crowd went crazy. Screaming and shouting and roaring in what might have been shock or outrage, they all surged determinedly *forward*. They wanted, they needed, to get to the stage, get to *her*. They fought each other with hands and elbows, snapping like animals. People were crushed, dragged down and trampled underfoot. Those nearest the dead man at the front tore him apart, literally limb from limb, scattering the bloody body parts among them like sacrificial offerings. There was an awful feeling of . . . celebration in the crowd. As though this was what they'd all been waiting for, even if they didn't know themselves.

I'd already vaulted up onto the stage and out of the way. Rossignol snapped out of her horrified daze, turned, and ran from the stage. The crowd saw her disappear and howled their rage and disapproval. They started to scramble up onto the stage. The backing singers ran forward to the edge of the stage and kicked viciously at people trying to pull themselves up. The three Ian Augers came forward and reinforced the singers with large, bony fists. But they were so few, and the crowd was so large, and so determined. Hell's Neanderthals waded into the crowd from the rear, slapping people down and throwing them in the direction of the exit, whether they wanted to go or not. I started after Rossignol. One of the Ian Augers reached out to grab me, but I've had a lot of practice at dodging un-

friendly hands. I headed backstage, just as the first
wave of the crowd boiled up over the edge.

Backstage, no-one tried to stop me. Everyone there
had their own problems, and once again as long as I
moved confidently and like I had a purpose and a right
to be there, no-one even looked at me. I saw the two
combat magicians coming and ducked through a side
door for a moment. They hurried past, dark sparks already sputtering around their fists as they prepared
themselves for some magical mayhem. They should be
able to hold off the crowd, assuming Stargrave and
Chance didn't get involved. If they did, there could be
some serious unpleasantness. I waited until I was sure
the combat magicians were gone, then headed for
Rossignol's dressing room.

She was sitting there alone, again, with her back to
the mirror this time. Her eyes were wild, unfocussed,
as she struggled to cope with what had just happened.
She was trying to scrub the blood and gore off her bare
feet with a hand towel. And yet, for all her obvious distress, it seemed to me that this was the most alive I'd
ever seen her. She looked up sharply as I came in and
shut the door behind me.

"Get out! Get out of here!"

"It's all right, Ross," I said quickly. "I'm not a fan."
I concentrated and shrugged off the seeming Pew had
placed on me. It was only a small magic, after all.
Rossignol recognised me as the tattoos disappeared
from my face, and she slumped tiredly.

"Thank God. I could use a friendly face."

She suddenly started to tremble, her whole body

shuddering, as the shock caught up with her. I took off my leather jacket and wrapped it gently round her shoulders. She grabbed my hands, squeezing them hard as though to draw some of my strength and warmth into her, then suddenly she was in my arms, holding me like a drowning woman, her tear-stained face pressed against my chest. I held her and comforted her as best I could. We all need a little simple human comfort, now and again. Finally, she let go, and I did, too. I knelt, picked up the hand towel, and cleaned the last of the blood off her feet to give her a moment to compose herself. By the time I'd finished and was looking around for somewhere to dump the towel, she seemed to have calmed down a little.

I straightened up, sat on the dressing room table, and dropped the towel beside me. "Has anything like this ever happened to you before, Ross?"

"No. Never. I mean, there have been rumours, but . . . no. Never right in front of me."

"Did you recognise the guy?"

"No! Never saw him before in my life! I don't mix with my . . . audience. The Cavendishes insist on that. Part of building the image, the mystique, they said. I never really believed the rumours . . . I thought it was just publicity, stories the Cavendishes put about to work up some excitement. I never dreamed . . ."

"As if we would ever do such a thing, dear Rossignol," said a cold, familiar voice behind me. I got to my feet and looked round, and there in the dressing room doorway were Mr. and Mrs. Cavendish. Tall and aristocratic, and twice as arrogant. They glided in like two dark birds of ill omen, ignoring their property Rossignol to consider me with a cold, thoughtful gaze.

"You do seem in very rude health, Mr. Taylor," said the man. "Does he not, Mrs. Cavendish?"

"Indeed he does, Mr. Cavendish. Quite the picture of good health."

"Perhaps some of the stories about you are true after all, Mr. Taylor."

I just smiled and said nothing. Let them wonder. It all added to the reputation.

"We did think you'd learned your lesson, Mr. Taylor," said the woman.

"Afraid not," I said. "I'm a very slow learner."

"Then we shall just have to try harder," said the man. "Won't we, Mrs. Cavendish?"

Rossignol was looking back and forth, confused. "You know each other?"

"Of course," said the man. "Everyone in the Nightside comes to us, eventually. Do not concern yourself, my dear. And most of all, do not worry yourself about the unfortunate incident during the show. Mrs. Cavendish and I will take care of everything. You must allow us to worry for you. That is what you pay us our forty per cent for."

"*How much?*" I said, honestly outraged.

"Our hard-won expertise does not come cheaply, Mr. Taylor," said the woman. "Not that it is any of your business. Isn't that correct, dear Rossignol?"

She seemed to shrink under their gaze, and she looked down at the floor like a scolded child. "Yes," she said, in a small voice. "That's right."

"What's happening out in the club?" I said.

"The club is being cleared," said the man. "It is a shame that the show had to be cut short, but we did make it clear on the tickets that there would be no refunds, under any circumstances."

"I am sure they will be back again, for the next show," said the woman. "Everyone is so desperate to hear dear Rossignol sing."

"You expect her to go on again, after what just happened?" I said.

"Of course," said the man. "The show must go on. And our dear Rossignol only lives to sing. Isn't that right, dear child?"

"Yes," said Rossignol, still staring at the floor. "I live to sing."

"People are dying!" I said loudly, trying to get a reaction from her. "Not just here, not just right now. This is only the most recent suicide, and the most public. People are taking their own lives because of what they hear when Rossignol sings!"

"Rumour," said the woman. "Speculation. Nothing more than tittle-tattle."

"And there will always be fanatics," said the man. "Poor deranged souls who fly too close to the flame that attracts them. You are not to concern yourself, dear Rossignol. The club will be cleared soon, and all will be made ready for your next performance. We will have extra security in place and take all the proper precautions to ensure your safety. Leave everything to us."

"Yes," said Rossignol. Her voice was heavy now, almost half-asleep. Just the presence of the Cavendishes had reduced her to the same dull state in which I'd first found her. There was no point in talking to her any more. So I shrugged mentally and took my jacket back from around her shoulders. She didn't react. I put it on, and the Cavendishes stepped back to make room for me to leave. I headed for the door like it was my decision, and the Cavendishes glided smoothly aside to let me pass. I was almost out of the room when Rossignol's voice stopped me. I looked back. She had her head up again, and her voice was quiet but determined.

"John, find out what's happening. I need to know the truth. Do this for me. Please."

"Sure," I said. "Saving damsels in distress is what I do."

SIX

All the News, Dammit

Every good guest knows better than to outstay his welcome. Especially if he's an uninvited guest, and his hosts want his head on a platter. So I slipped quietly away, passing unnoticed in the general chaos and hysteria backstage, and finally made my exit by a sinfully unguarded back door. The back alley was surprisingly clean and tidy, not to mention well lit, though I did surprise half a dozen of the cleaning monkeys caught up in a red-hot dice game. I murmured my apologies and hurried past them. Monkeys can get really nasty if you interrupt their winning streak.

I moved quietly round the corner of the club and peered down the side alley that led back to the main street. It was empty, for the moment, but there were clear sounds of trouble and associated mayhem out on the street. I padded cautiously forward, sneaking the occasional quick look over my shoulder, and eventually eased up to the front corner of Caliban's Cavern. Someone had already smashed the street-light there, so I stood and watched from the shadows as a riot swiftly put itself together outside the nightclub.

Out in front of Caliban's Cavern, a loud and very angry crowd was busily escalating a commotion into an open brawl. The recently ejected audience was feeling distinctly put upon and out of sorts at being cheated out of their show, and even more upset at the management's firm *no refunds* policy. A few of the crowd, most definitely including the various celebrities, were not at all used to being manhandled in such a peremptory manner, and many had taken it upon themselves to express their displeasure by tearing apart the whole front edifice of the club. Windows were smashed, facia torn away, and anything at all fragile ended up in small pieces all over the pavement. The outnumbered security staff retreated back inside the club and locked the front doors. The increasingly angry crowd took that as a challenge and set about kicking the doors in. Some even levered up bits of the pavement to use as missiles or battering rams.

An even larger crowd gathered, to watch the first crowd. Free entertainment was always highly valued in the Nightside, especially when it involved violence and the chance of open mayhem. On learning the reason for the riot, some of the new arrivals expressed their solidarity by joining in, and soon an army of angry faces were attacking the front of Caliban's Cavern with anything that came to hand. And it's surprising how many really destructive things can just come to hand, in the Nightside.

A roar of rabid motorcycles announced the arrival of security reinforcements. The outer edges of the huge seething mob looked round to see a pack of almost a hundred Hell's Neanderthals slamming to a halt on their stripped-down chopper bikes. They quickly dismounted and surged forward, howling their pre-verbal war cries and brandishing all sorts of simple weaponry. The mob turned to face them, happy and eager for a chance to have living targets to take out their fury on. The two sides joined battle with equal fervour, and soon half the street was a war zone, with bodies flying this way and that, and blood flowing thickly in the gutters. The watching crowd retreated to a safe distance and booed the newly arrived security for the spoilsports they were.

It seemed to me that this was a good time to make myself scarce, while the Cavendishes' attention would be focussed on more immediate problems. I skirted round the edges of the boiling violence, firmly resisting all invitations to become involved, and walked briskly back towards the business area of Uptown. I'd thought of someone else to go to in search of answers. When in doubt, go to the people who know everything, even if they can't prove any of it. Namely journalists, gossip columnists, and all the other nosey parkers employed by the *Night Times*, the Nightside's very own newspaper.

It didn't take long to reach Victoria House, the large and comfortably run-down building that housed the

Night Times. It was a big and bulky building because it had to be. Within its heavy grey stone walls the paper was written, edited, published, printed, and distributed every twenty-four hours, all under the guardianship of its remarkable owner and editor, Julien Advent. The legendary Victorian Adventurer himself. Advent had to keep everything under one roof because that was the only way he could ensure the paper's safety and independence. I paused outside the front door to look up at the gargoyles sneering down from the roof. One of them was scratching itself listlessly, but otherwise they showed no interest in me. I took that as a good sign. The gargoyles were always the first to make it clear when you were out of favour with the paper, and some of them had uncanny aim and absolutely no inhibitions when it came to bodily functions.

The *Night Times* has prided itself throughout its long history in telling the truth, the whole truth, and as much gossip as it could get away with it. This had not endeared it to the Nightside's many powerful movers and shakers, and they had all made attempts, down the years, to shut the paper down by magic, muscle, political and business pressure. But the *Night Times* was still going strong, over two centuries old now, and as determined as ever to tell the general populace where the bodies were buried. Sometimes literally. It helped that the paper had almost as many friends and admirers as enemies. The last time some foolish soul tried to interfere with the *Night Times*'s distribution, by sending out a small army of thugs to intimidate the news vendors, the Little Sisters of the Immaculate Chain Saw had made one of their rare public appearances to deal with the matter and made such a mess of the thugs it was three days before the gutters ran freely again.

I stepped up to the front door very carefully, ready to duck and run at a moment's notice. I was usually welcome at the *Night Times* offices, but it paid to be cautious. Victoria House had really heavy-duty magical defences, of a thorough and downright vicious nature that would have put the Cavendishes' defences to shame. They'd been built up in layers over two hundred years, like a malevolent onion. A subsonic avoidance spell ensured that most people couldn't even get close to the building unless they were on the approved list, or had legitimate business there. I'm not saying I couldn't get in if I really had to, but nothing short of a gun at the back of my head would convince me to try. The last time some idiot tried to smuggle a bomb into Victoria House, the defences turned him into something. No-one was quite sure what, because you couldn't look at him for more than a moment or two without projectile vomiting everything you'd ever eaten, including in previous lives. I'm told he, or more properly it, works in the sewer systems these days, and the rat population is way, way down.

I pushed the front door open, tensed, then relaxed as nothing awful happened to me. I counted my fingers anyway, just in case, and then strode into the lobby, smiling like I didn't have a care or guilty secret in the world. It's important to keep up appearances, especially in front of journalists. It was a wide-open lobby, to allow for a clean line of fire from as many directions as possible, and the receptionist sat inside a cubicle of bulletproof glass, surrounded by a pentacle of softly glowing blue lines. It was said by many, and believed by most, that you could nuke the whole building and the receptionist would still be okay.

The old dear put down her knitting as she saw me coming, studied me over the top of her granny glasses, and smiled sweetly. Most people thought of her as a nice old thing, but I happened to know that her knitting needles had been carved from human thigh-bones, and if she smiled widely enough, you could see that all her teeth had been filed to points.

"Ah, hello there, Mr. Taylor. So nice to see you back again. You're looking very yourself. Would I be right in thinking you're here to have a wee word with the man himself?"

"That's right, Janet. Could you ring up and ask Julien if he'll see me?"

"Oh, there's no need for that, you wee scamp. News of your latest exploits has already reached Mr. Advent, and he is most anxious to get all the details from you while they're still fresh in your mind." She shook her grey head and tut-tutted sadly. "Such a naughty boy you are, Mr. Taylor, always getting into trouble."

I just smiled and nodded, though I wasn't all that sure what she was talking about. Surely Julien couldn't know about my part in the destruction of Prometheus Inc. already? Janet hit the concealed switch that opened the elevator doors at the back of the lobby. She was the only one who could open the doors from this side, and she took her responsibility very seriously. There were those who said she never left her cubicle. Certainly no-one else had ever been seen in her place. I walked across the lobby, carefully not hurrying in case it made me look too anxious, and stepped into the waiting elevator. The steel doors closed silently, and I hit the button for the top floor.

Top floor was Editorial. I'd been there often enough before that my unexpected appearance shouldn't ring too many alarm bells. I used to do occasional legwork for the editor, in my younger days, before I had to leave the Nightside in a hurry. My gift for finding things came in very handy when Julien Advent needed to track down witnesses or people in hiding. I hadn't done anything for him recently, but he did still owe me a couple of favours . . . Not that I'd press the point. In the past, I'd always been careful to keep our relationship strictly business, because the great Victorian Adventurer had always been a man of unimpeachable and righteous morality, and such people have always made me very nervous. They tend not to approve of people like me, once they get to know me.

I'd never been sure how much Julien knew about my various dubious enterprises. And I've never liked to ask.

The elevator doors opened with a bright and cheerful chiming sound, and I stepped out into the plain, largely empty corridor that led to Editorial. The only decoration consisted of famous front pages from the *Night Times*'s long history, carefully preserved behind glass. Most were from way before my time, but I glanced at some of the more recent examples as I headed for the Editorial bullpen. *Angel War Ends in Draw, Beltane Blood Bonanza, New Chastity Scare, Who Watches the Authorities?* And, from its brief tabloid incarnation, *Sandra Chance Ate My Haploids!* (Julien Advent had been on vacation that month.) I stopped outside the bullpen to consider the *Night*

Times's famous motto, proudly emblazoned over the door.

ALL THE NEWS, DAMMIT.

The solid steel door had a wild mixture of protective runes and sigils engraved into its surface. It was sealed on all kinds of levels, but it recognised me immediately and opened politely. The general bedlam from within hit my ears like a thunderclap, and I braced myself before walking in like I had every right to be there. The long room was full of people, working at desks and shouting at each other. A few people ran back and forth between the desks, carrying important memos and updates, and the even more important hot coffee that kept everybody going. The bullpen ran at full blast, nonstop, in three eight-hour shifts, to be sure of covering everything as it happened. The computers were never turned off, and the seats were always warm. A few people looked round as I entered, smiled or grimaced, and went straight back to work. This wasn't a place for hanging around watercoolers—everyone here took their work very seriously.

The place hadn't changed at all in the five years I'd been away. It was still a mess. Desks groaned under the weight of computer equipment, tottering stacks of books, and assorted magical and high-tech paraphernalia. Piles of paper overflowed the In and Out trays, and the phones never stopped ringing. Ever-changing displays on the far wall showed the current times and dates within all the Timeslips operating within the Nightside, while a large map showed the constantly contracting and expanding boundaries of the Nightside itself. Occasional details within the map flickered on and off like blinking eyes, as reality rewrote itself.

Slow-moving ceiling fans did their best to move the cigarette smoke around. No-one had ever tried to ban smoking here—journalism in the Nightside was a high-stress occupation.

I breezed down the central aisle, nodding and smiling to familiar faces, most of whom ignored me. Junior reporters brushed past me as they scurried back and forth, trying to outshout each other. A zone of magical silence surrounded the communications section, cut off from the rest of the room as they chased up the very latest stories on telephones, crystal balls, and wax effigies. I stopped as the copyboy came whirling towards me. Otto was an amiable young poltergeist who manifested as a tightly controlled whirlwind. He bobbed up and down before me like a miniature tornado, tossing the papers he carried inside himself towards In trays and waiting hands with uncanny accuracy.

"Hello, hello, Mr. Taylor! So nice to have you back among us. Love the jacket. You here to see the gaffer, are you?"

"Got it in one, Otto. Is he in?"

"Well, that's the question, isn't it? He's in his office, but whether he's in to you . . . Hang on here while I nip in and check."

He shot off towards the soundproofed glass cubicle at the end of the bullpen, singing snatches of show tunes as he went. I could just make out Julien Advent sitting behind his editor's desk, making hurried last-minute corrections to a story, while his sub-editor hovered frantically before him. Julien finally finished, and the sub snatched the pages from the desk and ran for the presses. Julien looked up as Otto swirled into his office, then looked round at me.

I looked around the bullpen. Hardly anyone looked back. Despite all my previous hard work for the *Night Times*, they didn't consider me one of them. I didn't share their holy quest for pursuing news. And as far as newsies were concerned, it was always going to be them versus everyone else. You couldn't afford to get close to someone you might have to do a story on someday.

Not all of the staff were human. The editor operated a strictly equal opportunity employment programme. A semi-transparent ghost was talking to the spirit world on the memory of an old-fashioned telephone. Two ravens called Truth and Memory fluttered back and forth across the room. They were moonlighting from their usual job, working as fact-checkers. A goblin drag queen was working out the next day's horoscopes. His fluffy blonde wig clashed with his horns. It probably helped in his job that he was a manic depressive with a nasty sense of humour. His column might be occasionally distressing, but it was never boring. He nodded casually to me, and I wandered over to join him. He adjusted the fall of his bright green cocktail dress and smiled widely.

"See you, John! Who's been a naughty boy, then? That creep Walker was here looking for you earlier, and he was not a happy bunny."

"When is he ever?" I said calmly. "I'm sure it's all a misunderstanding. Any idea why the editor wants to see me?"

"He hasn't said, but then he never does. What have you been up to?"

"Oh, this and that. Anything in the future I should know about?"

"You tell me, pet. I just work here."

We shared a laugh, and he went back to scowling over his next column, putting together something really upsetting for tomorrow's Virgos. I strolled down the central aisle towards the editor's cubicle, as slowly as I thought I could get away with. There was no telling what Julien knew, or thought he knew, but I had no intention of telling him anything I didn't have to. Knowledge was power here, just as in the rest of the Nightside. A lot of the staff were affecting not to notice my presence, but I'm used to that. The haunted typewriter clacked busily away to my left, operated by a journalist who was murdered several years ago, but hadn't let a little thing like being dead interfere with his work. One of the *Night Times*'s few real ghost writers.

I'd almost reached the editor's cubicle, when the paper's gossip columnist pushed his chair back to block my way. Argus of the Thousand Eyes was a shape-shifter. He could be anyone or anything, and as a result was able to infiltrate even the most closely guarded parties. He saw everything, overheard all, and told most of it. He had an endless curiosity and absolutely no sense of shame. The number of death threats he got every week outnumbered those of all the rest of the staff put together. Which was probably why Argus had never been known to reveal his true shape or identity to anyone. Rumours of his complicated sex life were scandalous. For the moment he was impersonating that famous reporter Clark Kent, as played by Christopher Reeve in the *Superman* movies.

"So tell me," he said. "Is it true, about Suzie Shooter?"

"Probably," I said. "Who's she supposed to have killed now?"

"Oh, it's something much more juicy than that. According to a very reliable source, dear Suzie has been hiding some really delicious secrets about her family . . ."

"Don't go there," I said flatly. "Or if Suzie doesn't kill you, I will."

He sneered at me and changed abruptly into an exact copy of me. "Maybe I should go and ask her yourself."

I gripped him firmly by the throat and lifted him out of his chair, so I could stick my face right into his. Or, rather, mine. "Don't," I said. "It isn't healthy to be me at the best of times, and I don't need you muddying my waters."

"Put him down, John," said Julien Advent. I looked round, and he was standing in the open door of his cubicle. "You know you can't kill him with anything less than a flamethrower. Now get in here. I want a word with you."

I dropped Argus back into his chair. He stuck out my tongue at me and changed into an exact copy of Walker. I made a mental note to purchase a flamethrower and went over to join Julien in his office. He shut the door firmly behind me, then waved me to the visitor's chair. We both sat down and considered each other thoughtfully.

"Love the jacket, John," he said finally. "It's so not you."

"This from a man who hasn't changed his look since the nineteenth century."

Julien Advent smiled, and I smiled back. We might never be friends, or really approve of each other, but somehow we always got along okay. It probably helped that we had a lot of enemies in common.

Julien Advent was the Victorian Adventurer, the greatest hero of his age. Valiant and daring, he'd fought all the evils of Queen Victoria's time and never once looked like losing. He was tall and lithely muscular, impossibly graceful in an utterly masculine way, with jet-black hair and eyes, and an unfashionably pale face. Handsome as any movie star, the effect was somewhat spoiled by his unwaveringly serious gaze and grim smile. Julien always looked like he didn't believe in frivolous things like fun or movie stars. He still wore the stark black-and-white formal dress of his time, the only splash of colour a purple cravat at his throat, held in place by a silver pin presented to him by Queen Victoria herself. And it had to be said, Julien looked a damn sight more elegant than the Jonah. Julien had style.

There were any number of books and movies and even a television series about the great Victorian Adventurer, most of them conspiracy theories as to why he'd disappeared so suddenly, at the height of his fame, in 1888. And then he astonished everyone by reappearing out of a Timeslip into the Nightside in 1966. It turned out he'd been betrayed by the only woman he ever loved, who lured him into a trap set by his greatest enemies, the evil husband-and-wife team known as the Murder Masques. The three of them tricked him into a pre-prepared Timeslip, and the next thing he knew he'd been catapulted into the future.

Being the great man that he was, Julien Advent soon found his feet again. He went to work as a journalist for the *Night Times* and made a great investigative re-

porter—partly because he wasn't afraid or impressed
by anyone and partly because he had an even scarier
reputation than the villains he pursued so relentlessly.
Julien still fought evil and punished the guilty—he just
did it in a new way. He was helped in adjusting to his
new time by his newfound wealth. He'd left money in
a secret bank account, when he disappeared from 1888,
and the wonders of compound interest meant he'd
never have to worry about money ever again. Eventually Julien became the editor, then the owner, of the
Night Times, and that great crusading newspaper had
become the official conscience of the Nightside and a
pain in the arse to all those who liked things just fine
the way they were.

Still, everybody read the *Night Times*, if only to be
sure they weren't in it.

Julien Advent was in every way a self-made man.
He hadn't started out as a hero and adventurer. He was
just a minor research chemist, pottering away in a small
laboratory on a modest stipend. But somehow he created a transformational potion like no other, a mysterious new compound that could unlock the secret
extremes of the human mind. A potion that could make
a man absolute good or utter evil. He could have become a monster, a creature that lived only to indulge itself with all manner of violence and vice, but being the
good and moral man that he was, Julien Advent took
the potion and became a hero. Tall and strong, fast-
moving and quick-thinking, courageous and magnificent and unwaveringly gallant, he became the foremost
adventurer of his time.

A man so perfect, he'd be unbearable if he wasn't so
charming. He had tried to re-create his formula over the

years, but to no success. Some unknown ingredient escaped him, some unknown impurity in one of the original salts . . . and Julien Advent remained the only one of his kind.

He never did discover what happened to the Murder Masques. That terrible husband-and-wife team, who ran all the organised crime in the Victorian Nightside, their faces hidden behind red leather masks, were long gone . . . no more now than a footnote in history. Only really remembered at all as the main adversaries of the legendary Victorian Adventurer. Some said progress changed London and the Nightside so quickly that they couldn't keep up, or they were brought down by others of their vicious kind. And some said they just got old and tired and slow, and younger wolves dragged them down. Julien had tried to determine their fate, using all the considerable resources of the *Night Times*, but the Murder Masques were lost in the mists of history and legend.

The woman who betrayed Julien to his mortal enemies hadn't even made it into the legends, her very name forgotten. Julien had been known to say that that was the best possible punishment he could have wished for her. Otherwise, he never spoke of her at all.

And now he sat behind his editor's desk, studying me intently with his dark eyes and sardonic smile. Julien was still a man who saw the world strictly in black and white, and despite all his experience of life in the current-day Nightside, he still would have no truck with shades of grey. As a result, he was often not at all sure what to make of me.

"I'm putting together a piece on the recent unexpected power cuts," he said abruptly. "You wouldn't know anything about them, of course."

"Of course."

"And Walker's appearance here looking for you with fire and brimstone in his eyes was nothing but a coincidence."

"Couldn't have put it better myself, Julien. I'm all tied up with a new case at the moment, investigating the Cavendishes."

Julien frowned briefly. "Ah yes, the reclusive Mr. and Mrs. Cavendish. A bad pair, though always somehow just on the right side of the law. For all their undoubted influence in the Nightside, all I have on them are rumours and unsubstantiated gossip. Probably time I did another piece on them, just to see what nastiness they're involved with these days. They haven't sued me in ages. But don't change the subject, John. Why is Walker after you?"

"Don't ask me," I said, radiating sincerity. "Walker's always after me for something, you know that. Are you going to tell him I was here?"

Julien laughed. "Hardly, dear boy. I disapprove of him even more than I do of you. The man has far too much power and far too little judgement in the exercising of it. I honestly believe he has no moral compass at all. One of these days I'll get the goods on him, then I'll put out a special edition all about him. I did ask him if he knew what was behind the blackouts, but he wouldn't say anything. He knows more than he's telling . . . but then, he always does."

"How bad were the blackouts?" I asked cautiously.

"Bad. Almost half the Nightside had interruptions in their power supply, some of them disastrously so. Millions of pounds' worth of damage and lost business, and thousands of injuries. No actual deaths have been confirmed yet, but new reports are coming in all the time. Whoever was responsible for this hit the Night-side where it hurt. We weren't affected, of course. Victoria House has its own generator. All part of being independent. You were seen at Prometheus Inc., John, just before it all went bang."

I shrugged easily. "There'd been some talk of sabotage, and I was called in as a security consultant. But they left it far too late. I was lucky to get out alive."

"And the saboteur?"

I shrugged again. "We'll probably never know now."

Julien sighed tiredly. "You never could lie to me worth a damn, John."

"I know," I said. "But that is my official line as to what happened, and I'm sticking to it."

He fixed me with his steady thoughtful gaze. "I could put all kinds of pressure on you, John."

I grinned. "You could try."

We both laughed quietly together, then the door banged open suddenly as Otto came whirling in, his bobbing windy self crackling with energy. An eight-by-ten shot out of somewhere within him and slapped down on the table in front of Julien. "Sorry to interrupt, sir, but the pictures sub wants to know whether this photo of Walker will do for the next edition."

Julien barely glanced at the photo. "No. He doesn't look nearly shifty enough. Tell the sub to dig through the photo archives and come up with something that will make Walker look actually dishonest. Shouldn't be too difficult."

"No problem, chief."

Otto snatched the photo back into himself and shot out of the office, slamming the door behind him.

I decided Julien could use distracting from thoughts about Prometheus Inc., so I told him I'd been present at Caliban's Cavern when one of Rossignol's fans had shot himself right in front of her. Julien's face brightened immediately.

"You were there? Did you see the riot as well?"

"Right there on the spot, Julien. I saw it all."

And then, of course, nothing would do but I sit down with one of his reporters immediately and tell them everything while the details were still fresh in my mind. I went along with it, partly because I needed to keep Julien distracted, and partly because I was going to have to ask him a favour before I left, and I wanted him feeling obligated towards me. Julien's always been very big on obligation and paying off debts. I tend not to be. Julien used his intercom to summon a reporter to his office, a young up-and-comer called Annabella Peters. I tried to hide my unease. I knew Annabella, and she knew far too much about me. She'd already published several pieces on my return to the Nightside, after five years away, and she had speculated extensively about the reasons for my return, and all the possible consequences for the Nightside. Some of her guesses had been disturbingly accurate. She came barging into Julien's office with a mini tape recorder at the ready, a bright young thing dressed in variously coloured woollens, with a long face, a horsey smile and a sharp, remorseless gaze. She took my offered hand and pumped it briskly.

"John Taylor! Good to see, good to see! Always happy to have a little sit down and chat with you."

"Really?" I said. "In your last piece, you said I was a menace to the stability of the whole Nightside."

"Well, you are," she said reasonably. "What were you doing at Prometheus Inc., John?"

"We've moved on from that," I said firmly. "This is about the riot at Caliban's Cavern."

"Oh, the Rossignol suicide! Yes! Marvelous stuff, marvelous stuff! Did she really get his brains all over her feet?"

"Bad news travels fast," I observed. Annabella sat down opposite me and turned her recorder on. I told her the story, while downplaying my own involvement as much as possible. I suggested, as strongly as I could without being too obvious about it, that I was only there as part of my investigation of the Cavendishes, and not because of Rossignol at all. I never discuss my cases with journalists. Besides, putting the Cavendishes in the frame as the villains of the piece would make it easier for me when I had to ask Julien for that favour. The two of us had worked together in the past, on a few cases where our interests merged, but it never came easily. I finished my story of the riot by telling how I'd been swept outside along with the rest of the ejected audience and only saw the resulting mayhem from a safe distance. Julien nodded, as though he'd expected nothing else from me. Annabella turned off her mini recorder and smiled brightly.

"Thanks awfully, John. This will make a super piece, once I've chopped it down to a reasonable length. Pity you weren't more personally involved with the violence, though."

"Sorry," I said. "I'll try harder next time."

"One last question . . ." She surreptitiously turned

her recorder back on again, and I pretended I hadn't noticed. "There are rumours circulating, suggesting the Nightside was originally created for a specific purpose, and that this is somehow connected with your missing mother's true nature and identity. Could you add anything to these rumours?"

"Sorry," I said. "I never listen to gossip. If you do find out the truth, let me know."

Annabella sighed, turned off her recorder, and Julien held the door open for her as she left. She trotted off to write her piece, and Julien shut the door and came back to join me.

"You're not usually this cooperative with the press, John. Would I be right in assuming you're about to beg a favour from me?"

"Nothing that should trouble your conscience too much, Julien. It wouldn't break your heart if I was to bring the Cavendishes down, would it?"

"No. They're scum. Parasites. Their very presence corrupts the Nightside. Just like the Murder Masques in my day, only without the sense of style. But they're very big and very rich, and extremely well connected. What makes you think you can hurt them?"

"I may be onto something," I said carefully. "It concerns their new singer, Rossignol. What can you tell me about her?"

Julien considered for a moment, then used his intercom to summon the gossip columnist Argus. The shapeshifter breezed in, looking like Kylie Minogue. Dressed as a nun. She sat down beside me, adjusting her habit to show off a perfect bare leg. Julien glared at Argus, and she sat up straight and paid attention.

"Sorry, boss."

"Rossignol," said Julien, and that was all the prompting Argus needed.

"Well, I heard about the suicides, of course, everybody has, all of them supposedly linked to Rossignol's singing, but nobody's come forward with any real proof yet. For a long time we all thought it was just a publicity stunt. And, since no-one famous, or anyone who really matters, has died yet, the Authorities don't give a damn. They never do, until they're forced to. But . . . the word is that the Cavendishes have a lot riding on Rossignol's success. They need her to make it big. Really big. Their actual financial state is a lot dodgier than most people realise. A lot of their money was invested in property in the Nightside, most of which was thoroughly trashed during the recent Angel War. And of course insurance doesn't cover Acts of God. Or the Adversary. Or their angels. It was in the small print; the Cavendishes should have looked.

"Anyway, Rossignol is all set to be their new cash cow, and they can't afford to have anything go wrong with her big launch onto the music scene. Especially with what happened to their last attempt at creating a new singing sensation, Sylvia Sin. You wouldn't remember her, John. This was while you were still away. Sylvia Sin was going to be the new Big Thing. A marvelous voice, a face like an angel, and breasts to die for. She could whip up a crowd like no-one I ever saw. But she vanished, very mysteriously, just before her big opening night. Her current whereabouts are unknown. Lots of rumours, of course, but no-one's seen anything of her in over a year."

"She could have had it all," said Julien. "Fame, money, success. But something made her run away and dig a hole so deep no-one can find it. Which isn't easy, in the Nightside."

And that was when all hell broke loose out in the bullpen. All the supernatural-threat alarms went off at once, but it was already too late. Julien and I were immediately on our feet, staring out through the office's glass walls as a dark figure roared through the bullpen, throwing desks and tables aside, casually overturning and smashing computer equipment. Journalists and other staff dived for cover. Truth and Memory flew round the room, screeching loudly. Argus peered past my shoulder, her Kylie eyes wide. The dark figure paused for a moment, looking around for new targets, and it was only then that I realised it was Rossignol. She looked small and compact in her little black dress, and extremely dangerous. The expression on her face was utterly inhuman. She saw Julien and me watching, picked up a heavy wooden desk, and threw it the length of the bullpen. We scattered out of the way as the desk smashed through the cubicle's glass wall and flew on to slam against the opposite wall, before finally dropping to the floor with a crash.

Julien and I were quickly back at the shattered glass wall. Argus hid under the editor's desk.

"How the hell did she get in here, past all our defences?" Argus yelled.

"Language, please," Julien murmured, not looking round. "Only one answer—someone must have followed you here from the club, John. You brought her in with you."

"Oh come on, Julien. I think I would have noticed."

"That isn't Rossignol," Julien said firmly. "No-one human is that strong. That is a sending, probably from the Cavendishes, guided by something they planted on your person."

"No-one planted anything on me!" I said angrily. "No-one's that good!"

I searched my pockets anyway, paying special attention to the jacket Pew had given me, but there was nothing anywhere on me that shouldn't have been there. The fake Rossignol advanced menacingly on a group of journalists trying to build a barricade between themselves and her, and Julien decided he'd had enough. He strode out of his office and into the bullpen, heading straight for Rossignol. He might be an editor these days, but he was still every inch a hero. I hesitated, then went after him. I couldn't see how I might have brought that creature here, but Julien had made me feel responsible. He's good at that. Argus stayed in her hiding place.

Rossignol raged back and forth across the bullpen, smashing computer monitors with flashing blows of her tiny fists. The staff scattered back and forth, trying to keep out of her way. The ones that didn't got hurt. Her strength was enormous, impossible, as though she moved through a world made of paper. Her smile never wavered, and her eyes didn't blink. One journalist didn't move fast enough, and she grabbed him by the shoulder with one hand and slammed him against a wall so hard I heard his bones break. Julien was almost upon her. She dropped the limp body and turned suddenly to face him. She lashed out, and Julien only just dodged a blow that would have taken his head clean off his shoulders. Julien darted forward and hit her right on the point of the chin, and her head hardly moved with the blow.

Otto the poltergeist came bobbing over to join me, as I moved cautiously forward. "You've got to stop her, Mr. Taylor, before she destroys everything!"

"I'm open to suggestions," I said, wincing as another vicious blow only just missed Julien's head. "I'm a bit concerned that if we hurt or damage whatever the hell that thing is, we might hurt or damage the real thing."

"Oh, you don't have to worry about that," said Otto. "She's not real. Well, she is, in the sense that she's very definitely kicking the crap out of our revered editor right now, but that thing isn't in any way human. It's a tulpa, a thought form raised up in the shape of whatever person it's derived from. You must have brought something with you that came from the real Rossignol, something so small you didn't even notice."

I thought hard. I was sure Rossignol hadn't actually given me anything, which meant whatever it was must have been planted on me after all. I checked all my pockets again, and again came up with nothing. Julien was bobbing and weaving, snapping out punches that rocked the fake Rossignol back on her heels without actually hurting her. The goblin drag queen suddenly tackled Rossignol from behind and pinned her arms to her sides. Julien picked up a desk with an effort and broke it over her head. Rossignol didn't even flinch. She freed herself from the goblin's grasp with a vicious back elbow that left him gasping, and went after Julien again. She wasn't even breathing hard from her exertions. I decided, very reluctantly, that I was going to have to get involved.

I circled behind Rossignol, picked up a heavy paperweight, and bounced it off the back of her head. She spun round to face her new enemy, and Julien kicked her neatly behind her left knee. She staggered, caught off-balance, and Julien and I hit her together, putting all our strength into our blows. She just shrugged us off. We both backed away and circled her. She turned smoothly to keep us both in view. I looked around for something else to use and spotted a large bulky object with satisfyingly sharp points. Perfect. I reached for it, then hesitated as Annabella hissed angrily at me from behind an overturned table.

"Don't you dare, you bastard! That's my journalist of the year award!"

"Perfect," I said. I grabbed the ugly thing and threw it with all my strength. Rossignol snatched it out of mid air and threw it straight back, and it only just missed my head as I dived for cover. Julien yelled back at his office.

"Argus! Get your cowardly self out here! I've got an idea!"

"I don't care if you've got a bazooka, I'm not budging! You don't pay me enough to fight demons!"

"Get your miserable self out here, or I'll cut off your expenses!"

"Bully," said Argus, but not too loudly. He came slouching out of the editor's office, trying to look as anonymous as possible. His face was so bland as to be practically generic. He edged towards the ongoing battle, while Julien glared at him.

"Look like Rossignol! Do it now!"

Argus shapeshifted and became an exact copy of Rossignol. The tulpa looked at the new fake Rossignol and paused, bewildered. Julien caught my atten-

tion and gestured at an overturned table. I quickly
saw what he had in mind, and we picked it up between us. The tulpa Rossignol had just started to
come out of her trance when we hit her from behind
like a charging train. Caught off-balance, she fell forward, and we threw our combined weight onto the
table, pinning the tulpa to the ground. She struggled
underneath us, trying to find the leverage to free herself. And I used my gift and found just what it was
that the tulpa was using as its link. On the shoulder of
my jacket was a single black hair from Rossignol's
head, almost invisible against the black leather. It
must have happened when I held her in my arms to
comfort her. No good deed goes unpunished, especially in the Nightside. I held up the hair to show it to
Julien, while the table bucked beneath us. He produced a monogrammed gold lighter and set fire to the
hair. It burned up in a moment, then the table beneath
us slammed flat against the floor. There was no
longer anything underneath it.

Julien and I helped each other to our feet. We were
both breathing hard. He looked about his devastated
bullpen, as journalists and other staff slowly emerged
from the wreckage. Somebody found a phone that still
worked and called paramedics for the injured. Julien
looked at me, and his dark eyes were very cold.

"This has to be the Cavendishes' work. And that
makes this personal. No-one attacks the *Night Times*
and gets away with it. I think I'll send the arrogant
swine a bill for damages and repairs. Meanwhile, I'm
starting a full-scale investigation into what they're up
to, using all my best people. And John, I suggest you go

and see Dead Boy. If anyone knows where Sylvia Sin is hiding, it will be he."

I nodded. That was the favour I'd been hoping for.

Julien Advent looked back at his wrecked bullpen. "No-one attacks my people and gets away with it."

SEVEN

Death and Life, Sort of

I left the *Night Times* riding in Julien Advent's very own Silver Ghost Rolls-Royce. He wanted to make sure I got where I was going and not die anywhere near him or the *Night Times*'s offices. I considered this a thoughtful gesture and left him and the rest of the staff to clean up the extensive mess and damage caused by Rossignol's tulpa. My chauffeuse was a slender delicate little flower in a full white leather outfit, right down to the peaked chauffeur's hat pulled firmly down over her mop of frizzy golden hair. She asked me where she was to take me, then refused to say another word. I have that effect on women sometimes. Either that, or Julien had warned her about me. I sprawled happily on the polished red leather seat and indulged myself with a very good brandy from the built-in bar. It does the heart and soul good to travel first-class once in a while. The Rolls purred along, sliding smoothly through the packed and snarling traffic of the Nightside, where the only rule of the road is survival. Most of the other vehicles had enough sense to give the Rolls plenty of room—they knew that a vehicle that expensive had to have state-of-the-art defences and weaponry.

But there's always one, isn't there? I was peering vaguely out the side window, not really thinking about anything much, except trying to remember whether Dead Boy and I had parted on good terms the last time we'd met, when I gradually became aware of a battered dark saloon car of unfamiliar make easing in beside us. It didn't take me long to realise it wasn't a proper car. I sat up straight and paid attention. All the details were wrong, and when I looked closely, I could see that the car's wheels weren't turning at all. I looked at the chauffeuse. She was staring straight ahead, apparently not at all concerned. I looked at the black car again. The outlines of the doors were just marks on the chassis, with no depth to them, and though the back windows were opaque, I could see the driver through the front side window. He wasn't moving at all. I was pretty sure he was a corpse, just put there to add verisimilitude and fool the casual eye.

The Rolls was moving pretty fast, and so was the thing that wasn't a car. It really was getting very close. A split appeared in the side facing me, stretching slowly to reach from one end to the other. It opened like a mouth, revealing rows of bloodred cilia within, thrashing hungrily. They sprouted vicious barbs and lashed out at the Rolls's windows. I retreated to the opposite side of the seat, as the cilia scratched futilely at the bulletproof glass. The chauffeuse reached for the weapons console on the dashboard.

And then the fake car lurched suddenly, as huge feet slammed down from above, burying long claws in the fake roof. Blood spurted thickly from the wounds the claws made. The thing surged back and forth across the road, trying to break the claws' hold, and couldn't. Its wide mouth screamed shrilly as it was lifted suddenly up and off the road. There was the sound of very large leathery wings flapping, and the thing that only looked like a car was gone, snatched up into the night skies. It had made a very foolish mistake—in becoming so fascinated by its prey it forgot the first rule of the Nightside. No matter how good a predator you are, there's always something bigger and stronger and hungrier than you, and if you let yourself get distracted, it'll creep right up behind you.

The Rolls-Royce purred on its way, the traffic continued as though nothing had happened, and I drank more brandy.

It took about half an hour to reach the Nightside Necropolis, site of Dead Boy's current assignment. The Necropolis takes care of all funerals for those who die in the Nightside and is situated right out on the boundary, because no-one wanted to be too close to it. Partly because even the Nightside has some taboos, but mostly because on the few occasions when things go wrong at the Necropolis, they go *really* wrong.

It is the management's proud claim that they can

provide every kind of service, ritual, or interment you think of, including a few best not thought of at all if you like sleeping at night. Their motto: It's *Your* Funeral. In the Nightside, you can't always be sure that the dear departed will rest in peace, unless the proper precautions are taken, so it pays to have professionals who specialise in such matters. They charge an arm and a leg, but they can work wonders, even when there isn't an actual body for them to work with.

So when things do go wrong, as they will in even the best regulated firms, they tend to go spectacularly wrong, and that's when the Necopolis management swallows its considerable pride and calls in the Nightside's very own expert in all forms of death—the infamous Dead Boy.

The chauffeuse brought the Rolls to a halt a respectful distance away from the Necropolis. In fact, I could only just make out the building at the end of the street. I'd barely got out of the car and slammed the door shut behind me before the Rolls was backing away at speed, heading back to the more familiar dangers of Uptown. Which if nothing else solved the nagging problem of whether I was supposed to tip the chauffeuse. I've never been very good at working out things like that. I set off down the street, which was very quiet and utterly deserted. All the doors and windows were shut, and there were no lights on anywhere. My footsteps sounded loud and carrying, letting everyone know I was coming.

By the time I got to the Necropolis building itself, my nerves were absolutely ragged, and I was ready to jump right out of my skin at the first unexpected movement. The huge towering edifice before me was built of old brick and stone, with no windows anywhere, and a long sharp-edged gabled roof. It had been added to and extended in all directions, down the long years, and now it sprawled over a large area, the various contrasting styles not even trying to get along with each other. It was a dark, lowering, depressing structure with only one entrance. The massive front door was solid steel, rimmed with silver, covered with deeply etched runes, sigils, and other dead languages. I pitied the poor sod who had to polish that every morning. Two huge chimneys peered over the arching roof, serving the crematorium at the back, but for once there was no black smoke pumping up into the night sky. There was also supposed to be a hell of a graveyard in the rear, but I'd never seen it. Never wanted to. I don't go to funerals. They only depress me. Even when my dad died, I only went to the service. I know too much about pain and loss to take any false comfort from planting people in the ground. Or maybe I've just seen too many people die, and you can't keep saying good-bye.

Dead Boy's car was parked right outside the front entrance, and I strolled over to it. Gravel crunched loudly under my feet as I approached Dead Boy's one known indulgence—his brightly gleaming silver car of the future. It was long and sleek and streamlined to within an inch of its life, and it had no wheels. It hovered a few inches above the ground and looked like it ran on liquid starlight. Probably had warp drive, deflector shields, and, if pushed, could transform itself into a bloody great robot. The long curving windows were polarized so you couldn't see in, but the right-hand front door was open. There was one leg protruding. It didn't move as I drew near, so I had to bend over and peer into the driving seat. Dead Boy smiled pleasantly back at me.

"John Taylor. So good to see you again. Welcome to the most popular location in the Nightside."

"Is it really?"

"Must be. People are dying to get into it."

He laughed and took a long drink from his whiskey bottle. Dead Boy was seventeen. He'd been seventeen for over thirty years, ever since he was murdered. I knew his story. Everybody did. He was killed in a random mugging, because such things do happen, even here in the Nightside. Clubbed to death in the street, for his credit cards and the spare change in his pockets. He bled to death on the pavement, while people stepped over and around him, not wanting to get involved. And that should have been it. But he came back from the dead, filled with fury and unnatural energies, to track down and kill the street trash who murdered him. They died, one by one, and did not rise again. Perhaps after all the awful things Dead Boy had done to them, Hell seemed like a relief. But though they were all dead and gone long ago, Dead Boy went on, still walking the Nightside, trapped by the deal he made.

Who did you make your deal with? He was often asked. *Who do you think?* he always replied.

He got his revenge, but nothing had ever been said in the deal he made about being able to lie down again afterwards. He really should have read the small print. And so he goes on, a soul trapped in a dead body. Essentially, he's possessing himself. He does good deeds because he has to. It's the only chance he has of breaking the compact he made. He's a useful sort to have on your side—he doesn't feel pain, he can take a hell of a lot of damage, and he isn't afraid of anything in this world.

He's spent a lot of time researching his condition. He knows more about death in all its forms than any-one else in the Nightside. Supposedly.

He got up out of his car to greet me, all long gangling legs and arms, then leaned languidly against the side of the car. He was tall and adolescent thin, wearing a long, deep purple greatcoat over black leather trousers and shining calfskin boots. He wore a black rose in one lapel. The coat hung open, revealing his bare scarred torso. Being the revived dead, his body doesn't decay, but neither does it heal, so when he gets damaged on a case, as he often does, having no sense of self-preservation, Dead Boy stitches, staples, and super-glues his corpse-pale flesh back together again. Occasionally, he has to resort to duct tape. It's not a pretty sight. There were recent bullet holes in his great-coat, but neither of us mentioned them.

His long pale face had a weary, debauched, pre-Raphaelite look, with burning fever-bright eyes and a sulky pouting mouth with no colour to it. He wore a large floppy black hat over long dark curly hair. He drank whiskey straight from the bottle and munched chocolate biscuits. He offered me both, but I declined.

"I don't need to eat or drink," Dead Boy said casu-ally. "I don't feel hunger or thirst, or even drunkenness any more. I just do it for the sensations. And since it's hard for me to feel much of anything, only the most ex-treme sensations will do." He produced a silver pill-box from inside his coat, spilled half a dozen assorted pills out onto his palm, and knocked them back with more whiskey. "Marvelous stuff. Little old Obeah woman makes them for me. It's not easy getting drugs strong enough to affect the dead. Please don't look at me like that, John. You always were an overly sensitive soul. What brings you to this charmless spot?"

"Julien Advent said you were working a case here. If I help you out, would you be willing to work with me on something?"

He considered the matter, eating another biscuit and absently brushing the crumbs off his lapels. "Maybe. Does your case involve danger, gratuitous violence, and kicking the crap out of the ungodly?"

"Almost certainly."

Dead Boy smiled. "Then consider us partners. Assuming we survive my current assignment, of course."

I nodded at the silent, brooding Necropolis. "What's happened here?"

"A good question. It seems the Necropolis suffered an unexpected power cut, and all hell broke loose. I've been telling them for years they should get their own generator and hang the expense, but . . . Anyway, the cryonics section was very badly hit. I warned them about setting that up, too, but oh no, they had to be up to date, up to the moment, ready to meet any demand their customers might come up with." He paused. "I did try it out myself, once, wondering whether I could sleep it out in the ice until someone found an answer to my predicament, but it didn't work. I didn't even feel the cold. Just lay there, bored . . . Took me ages to get the icicles out of my hair afterwards, as well."

I nodded like I was listening, but inside I was cursing silently. Another consequence of my actions at Prometheus Inc. No good deed goes unpunished . . .

If the cryonics section was the problem here, we

were in for a really rough ride. Bodies have to be dead before they can be frozen and preserved, which means the soul has already departed. However, since some people have a firm suspicion of where their souls might be headed, they see cryonics as their last hope. Get a necromancer in after the body dies, and have him perform the necessary rituals to tie the soul to the body. Then freeze it, and there they are, all safe and sound till Judgement Day. Or until the power cuts out. There were supposed to be all kinds of safe-guards, but . . . Once the power failed, all the frozen bodies would start defrosting, and the spell holding the souls to them would be short-circuited. So you'd end up with a whole bunch of untenanted thawing bodies, every one of them a ripe target for possession by outside forces.

"So," I said, trying hard to sound calm and casual and not all worried. "Do we know what's got into them?"

"Afraid not. Facts are a bit spotty. About two hours ago, everyone who worked here came running out screaming and refused to go back. Most just kept running. And given the appalling things they deal with here every day as a matter of course, I think we can safely assume the *oh shit* factor is way off the scale. According to the one member of the Necropolis management I talked to who wasn't entirely hysterical, we have five newly thawed bodies to deal with, all of them taken over by *Something From Outside*. Doesn't exactly narrow the field down, does it? The only good news is that the magical wards surrounding the Necropolis are still intact and holding. So whatever's in there is still in there."

"Can't we just turn the power back on?" I said hopefully.

Dead Boy gave me a pitying smile. "Try and keep up with the rest of us, John. Power was reconnected some time back, but the damage had been done. The corpsicles' new tenants have made themselves at home, and their influence now extends over the whole building. The Necropolis's own tame spellslingers have tried all the usual techniques for putting down unwanted visitors from Beyond, from a safe distance, of course, but it seems the possessors are no ordinary imps or demons. We're talking extra-dimensional creatures, elder gods, many-angled ones—the right bastards of the Outer Dark. Not the sort to be bothered by your everyday expulsions or exorcisms. No, something really nasty has taken advantage of the situation to wedge open a door into our reality, and if we don't figure out a way to slam it shut soon, there's no telling what might come howling through. So we get to go in there and serve the extradition papers in person. Aren't we the lucky ones?"

"Luck isn't quite the word I was going to use," I said, and he laughed, entirely unconcerned.

I looked down at the ground before me. A narrow white line crossed the gravel, marking the boundary of the protective wards surrounding the Necropolis. It had been laid down in salt and silver and semen centuries before, to keep things in and keep things out. It remained unbroken, which was a good sign. Those old-time necromancers knew their business. I crouched down and touched the white line with a tentative fingertip. Immediately I could feel the presence of the force wall, like an endless roll of thunder shaking the air. I could also feel a great pressure, pushing constantly from the other side. Something wanted out bad. It was raging at the wall that held it imprisoned, and it was getting stronger all the time. I snatched my hand back and straightened up again.

"Oh yes," said Dead Boy, draining the last of his whiskey and throwing the bottle aside. "Nasty, isn't it?" The bottle smashed on the gravel, but the sound seemed very small. Dead Boy fixed the front door of the Necropolis with a speculative look. "Any ward will go down, if you hit it hard enough and long enough. So it's up to thee and me to go in there and clean their extra-dimensional clocks, while there's still time. Ah me, I do so love a challenge! Stop looking at me like that, it's going to be fun! Stick close to me, John. The charm the management gave me will get us past the wards, but it won't let you out again if we get separated."

"Don't worry," I said. "I'll be right behind you. Hiding."

Dead Boy laughed, and we crossed the barrier together.

It hit us both at the same time, a psychic assault so powerful and so vile we both staggered and almost fell. Something was watching us, from behind the blind, windowless walls of the Necropolis. A presence permeated the atmosphere, hanging on the air like an almost palpable fog, something dark and awful and utterly alien to human ways of thinking. It felt like crying and vomiting and the smell of your own blood, and it throbbed with hate. Approaching the Necropolis was like wading through an ocean of shit while someone you loved thrust knives into your face. Dead Boy just straightened his shoulders and took it in his stride, heading directly for the front door. I suppose there's nothing like having already died to put everything else in perspective. I gritted my teeth, hugged myself tightly to keep from falling apart, and stumbled forward into the teeth of the psychic assault.

We got to the door without anything nasty actually turning up to rip chunks off us, and Dead Boy rattled the door handle. From his expression, I gathered it wasn't supposed to be locked. He pushed at it with one hand, and it didn't budge. Dead Boy pulled back his hand and looked at it thoughtfully. I put my hand against the solid steel door, and it gave spongily, as though the substance, the reality of it, was being slowly leached out of it. My skin crawled at the contact, and I snatched my hand back and rubbed it thoroughly against my jacket. Dead Boy raised one booted foot and kicked the door in. The great slab of steel and silver flew inwards as though it were weightless, torn away from its hinges. It fell forward and slapped against the floor inside, making a soft, flat sound. Dead Boy strode over it into the entrance hall beyond. I hurried in after him as he struck a defiant pose, hands on hips, and glared into the gloom ahead of him.

"Hello there! I am Dead Boy! Come out here so I can kick your sorry arse! Go on, give me your best shot! I can take it!"

"You see?" I said. "This is why other people don't want to work with you."

"Bunch of wimps," he said, indifferently.

The smell was really bad. Blood and rot and the

scent of things that really belonged inside the body.
The only light in the great open hall came from a thin,
shifting mist that curled slowly on the air, glowing
blue-silver like phosphorescence. My eyes slowly adjusted to the dim light, then I wished they hadn't as for
the first time I saw the walls, and what was on them.
All around us, the walls were covered with a layer of
human remains. Corpses had been stretched and flat-
tened and plastered over the walls from floor to ceiling,
layering the hall with an insulating barrier of human
skin and guts and fractured bones. There were hundreds, thousands of distorted faces, from bodies presumably torn from the graveyard out back. The human
remains had been given a kind of life. They stirred
slowly as they became aware of us. Eyes rolled in
tightly spread faces, tracking the two of us as we advanced slowly across the great open hall. Hands and
arms stretched out from the walls as though to grab us,
or appeal for help. I could see hearts and lungs, pulsing
and swelling in a mockery of life. I was just glad I didn't
recognise any of the faces.

At least the floor was clear. Dead Boy strode forward, not even glancing at the walls, and I went with
him. I felt somebody sane should be present when push
inevitably came to shove. The sound of our feet on the
bare floor was strangely muffled, and the shadows
around us were very dark and very deep. It felt like
walking down a tunnel, away from our world and its
rules into . . . somewhere else.

We were almost half-way across the hall before we
got our first glimpse of what was waiting for us. At the
far end, in the darkest of the shadows, barely illuminated by the light of the swirling mists, were five huge

figures. The corpsicles. Thawed from unimaginable cold, revived from the dead, reanimated by abhuman spirits from Outside, they didn't look human any more. The forces that possessed the vacant bodies were too strong, too furious, too *other* for merely human frames to contain. They had all grown and expanded, forced into unnatural shapes and configurations by the pressures within, and now they were changed and mutated in hideous ways. It hurt to look at them. Their outlines seethed and fluctuated, trying to contain more than three dimensions at once. Mere flesh and blood and bone should have broken down and fallen apart, but the five abominations were held together by the implacable will of the creatures possessing them. They needed these bodies, these vacant hosts. The corpsicles were their only means of access to the material world. I kept wanting to look away. The shapes the bodies were trying to take were just too complex, too intricate for simple human minds to deal with.

We were getting too close. I grabbed Dead Boy by the arm and made him stop. He glared at me.

"We need information," I murmured. "Talk to them."

"You talk to them. Find me something useful I can hit."

One of the shapes leaned forward. It was twice as tall as a man, and almost as wide, its pale, sweating skin stretched painfully tight. A head craned forward on the end of a long, extended neck. Bloody tears fell constantly, to hiss and steam on the hall floor. Bone horns and antlers thrust out of the distorted face, and, when it spoke, its voice was like a choir of children whispering obscenities.

"We are The Primal. Purely conceptual beings, products of the earliest days of creation, before the glory of ideas was trapped and diminished in the narrow confines of matter. Kept out of the material worlds, to protect its fragile creatures of meat and mortality. Ever since Time was, we were. Waiting and watching at the Edge of things, searching eternally for a way in, to finally show our contempt and hatred for all the lesser creations, that dare to dream of being more than they are. We are The Primal. We were here first. And we will be here when all the meat that dares to think has been stamped back into the mud it came from."

"Typical bloody demons," said Dead Boy. "Created millennia ago, and still sulking because they didn't get better parts in the story. Let's get this over with. Come on, let's see what you can do!"

"Can you at least try for a more rational attitude?" I said sharply. And then I broke off, as the head turned suddenly to look at me.

"We know you, little prince," said the choir of whispering voices. "John Taylor. Yes. We know your mother, too."

"What do you know about her?" My mouth was painfully dry, but I fought to keep my voice steady.

"She who was first, and will be first again, in this worst of all possible worlds. She's coming back. Yes. Soon, she will come back."

"But who is she? What is she?"

"Ask the ones who called her up. Ask the ones who called her back. She is coming home, and she will not be denied."

"You're scared of her," I said, almost wonderingly. *And you're scared of me, too,* I thought.

"We are The Primal. There is still time to play in the world, before she comes back to take it for her own. Time to play with you, little prince."

"This is all terribly interesting," said Dead Boy. "But enough of the chit-chat. Back me up, John. I have a plan."

And he ran forward and threw himself at the nearest shape.

"That's your idea of a plan?" I shrieked, and plunged after him, because there was nothing else to do. It's times like this I wish I carried a gun. A really big gun. With nuclear bullets.

Dead Boy reached out to grab the extended head of the speaking Primal, and its whole body surged suddenly forward to engulf and envelop him, holding him firm like an insect in amber. It wanted to possess him, but Dead Boy was already possessing his body, and his curse didn't allow room for anyone else. The Primal convulsed and spat him out, repulsed by his very nature. Dead Boy hit the floor hard, but was back on his feet in a moment, looking around for something he could hit. The Primal raised their voices in a terrible harmony, chanting something in a language full of higher things than words. And the reanimated dead plastered across the walls heard them. They slipped slowly down the walls and slid across the floor towards Dead Boy and me, a sea of body parts oozing and undulating towards us from all directions, spitting and seething and sprouting distorted limbs like weapons. Stomach acids burned the wooden floor. Eyeballs rose up on wavering stalks. Hands flexed fingers with nails long as knives, sharp as scalpels.

I grabbed two handfuls of salt from my jacket

pocket and scattered it in a wide circle around Dead
Boy and myself, yelling to him to stay inside it. I
wasn't sure even his legendary invulnerability would
stand up to being torn apart and digested in a hundred
undead stomachs. The oozing biomass hesitated at the
salt, then formed itself into high, living arches to cross
over it. I glared about me, while Dead Boy slapped and
punched at the nearest extensions of the biomass. He
was shouting all kinds of spells, from elvish to corrupt
Coptic, but none of them had any obvious effect. The
reanimated tissues were charged with the energies of
The Primal, forces old when the world was new, and
even Dead Boy had never come across anything like
this before.

I looked at The Primal. They were watching me,
rather than Dead Boy, and I remembered my original
insight, that they'd seemed almost afraid of me. Why
me? What could I do to hurt them? I didn't even have
the few battle magics Dead Boy had. There was my gift
of finding, but I didn't see it being much use just then.
Think, think! I looked hard at the five distorted bodies
possessed by The Primal. They looked horrible, yes,
but also . . . strained, stretched thin, unstable. Human
bodies weren't meant to hold Primal essences. Maybe
all the pressure within needed was a little extra
nudge . . .

I was off and running even while the thought was
still forming in my mind, my feet slapping and sliding
on the slippery rotting organs beneath me. I headed
straight for the nearest shape, the speaking Primal,
shouting, "YOU THINK YOU'RE SO HARD, POS-
SESS ME, YOU BASTARDS!" while at the same time
thinking, *I really hope I'm right about this.* I hit the

first Primal even as it tried to draw back, and I slammed right into the heart of it. The body sucked me in like a mud pool, and I clapped a hand over my mouth and nose to keep it out. I felt cold, impossibly cold, like the dark void between the stars, but even worse than that, I could feel a vast and unknowable mind in there with me, in the cold and the dark, pressing upon me from all sides. And then suddenly there was screaming, an awful sound of outrage and betrayal, as the possessed body exploded.

I'd been too much for The Primal to manage. My body was still tenanted, soul intact, and The Primal couldn't cope. Something had to give, and it turned out to be the possessed body. It blew apart in a wet, sticky explosion, like a grenade inside a small furry creature, and the violence of the explosion ruptured the integrity of the four other bodies, setting them off like a row of firecrackers. It was all over in a moment, and Dead Boy and I stood looking around us, drenched in blood and gore, surrounded by a sea of unmoving body parts, already rotting and falling apart. Dead Boy looked at me.

"And people say I'm impulsive and hard to get along with. What did you just do to them?"

"I think I gave them indigestion. And, possibly, I am a bit special, after all."

Dead Boy sniffed. "God, I'm a mess. So are you. I really hope they've got some showers here somewhere. And a really good laundry."

Two long and very thorough showers later, Dead Boy and I climbed back into our very thoroughly laundered clothes. The Necropolis staff returned in dribs and

drabs once it was clear the danger was over, and, with
many a sigh and muttered oath, they began cleaning up
the mess. A slow process that involved body bags,
strong stomachs, not a little use of buckets and mops,
and a *really* big bottle of Lysol. The Necropolis management made a brief appearence, to shake our hands
and assure Dead Boy the cheque was in the post. They
meant it. Absolutely no-one wanted Dead Boy mad at
them. He tended to come round to where you lived and
pull it down around you. As Dead Boy and I were leaving the Necropolis, two young men were staggering in,
carrying a very large crate with the words *Air Freshen-
ers* stencilled on the side.

We headed for Dead Boy's car of the future, and the
doors swung open without being asked. Dead Boy
slipped in behind the wheel, and I sank carefully into
the luxurious front seat. The doors closed by themselves. The dashboard had more controls and displays
than the space shuttle. Dead Boy produced an Extra-
large Mars bar from somewhere and ate it in quick,
hungry mouthfuls. When he'd finished, he crumpled up
the wrapper and dropped it on the floor, where it joined
the rest of the junk. He stared moodily out the wind-
screen. He looked like he wanted to scowl, but couldn't
work up the energy.

"I'm tired," he said abruptly. "I'm always tired. And
I am so bloody tired of being tired. Everything's such
an effort, whether it's fighting elder gods or just getting
through another day. You have no idea what it's like,
being dead. I can't feel the subtle things any more, like
a breeze or a scent, or even hot and cold. I have no appetites or needs, and I never sleep. I can't even remember what it was like, to be able to put aside the cares of

the day and escape into oblivion, and dreams. Even my emotions are only shadows of what I remember them being like. It's hard to care about anything, when the worst thing that can happen to you has already happened. I just go on, doing my good deeds because I have no choice, throwing myself into danger over and over again for the chance to feel *something* . . . You sure you still want me to partner you, John?"

"I could use your help," I said. "And your insights. It's not much of a case, but it is . . . interesting."

"Ah well," said Dead Boy. "I can make do with interesting. Where are we going?"

"That's rather up to you. I'm looking for an ex-singer called Sylvia Sin. Used to be managed by the Cavendishes. Julien Advent thought you might know where she's hidden herself."

Dead Boy gave me a look I didn't immediately recognise. "I'm surprised you're interested in someone like her, John. Not really your scene, I would have thought. Still, far be it for me to pass judgement . . ."

"She's part of the case I'm working," I said. "Do you know where she is?"

"Yes. And I know what she's doing these days. You're wasting your time there, John. Sylvia Sin doesn't care about anyone or anything except what she does."

"I still have to talk to her," I said patiently. "Will you take me to her?"

He shrugged. "Why not? If nothing else, it should be interesting to see your face when we get there."

Dead Boy's car of the future slid smoothly through the Nightside traffic, all of which gave it plenty of room.

Probably afraid of phasers and photon torpedos. If the engine made a noise, I couldn't hear it, and the car handled like a dream. I couldn't feel the acceleration, even though we were moving faster than anything else on the road. All too soon we'd left the main flow of traffic behind and were cruising through the quiet back streets of a mostly residential area. We glided past rows of typically suburban houses and finally stopped in front of one that looked no different from any of the others. Even the Nightside has its quiet backwaters, and this was one of the quietest.

Dead Boy and I got out of the car, which locked itself behind us. I hunched inside my jacket against a slow sullen drizzle. The night had turned gloomy and overcast, with heavy clouds hiding the stars and the oversized moon. The yellow street-lights gave the scene a sick, sleazy look. There was no-one else around, and most of the houses had no lights showing. Dead Boy led the way through an overgrown garden and up to the front door, then stood aside and indicated for me to knock. Again, his expression was hard to read. There being no bell, I knocked, and the door opened immediately. As though someone had been watching, or waiting.

The man who opened the door might as well have had a neon sign hanging over his head saying *Pimp*. The way he looked, the way he stood, the way he smiled, all combined to make you feel welcome and dirty at the same time. He wore an oriental black silk wraparound, with a bright red Chinese dragon motif. He was short and slender, almost androgynous. There were heavy silver rings on all his fingers, and a silver ring pierced his left nostril. His jet-black hair was slicked back, and there was something subtly *wrong* about his face. Something in the angles, or perhaps in the way he held his head. He never stopped smiling, but the smile didn't touch his dark, knowing eyes.

"Always happy to see new faces," he said, in a light breathy voice. "All are welcome here. And such famous faces. The legendary Dead Boy, and the newly returned John Taylor. Honoured to make your acquaintance, sirs. My name is Grey, entirely at your service."

"We need to see Sylvia," said Dead Boy. "Or at least, John does."

"But of course," said Grey. "No-one ever comes here to see me." He turned his constant smile in my direction. "What's your pleasure, sir? Whatever you want, whoever you want, I can promise you'll find it here. Nothing is forbidden, and everything is encouraged. Dear Sylvia is always very accommodating."

"Don't I need an appointment?" I said. I shot Dead Boy a quick glare. He should have warned me.

"Oh, Sylvia always knows when someone is coming," said Grey. "As it happens, she's just finished with her last client. You can go straight up, once we've agreed on a suitable fee, of course. In an ideal world such vulgarity would be unnecessary, but alas . . ."

"I'm not interested in buying her services," I said. "I just need to talk to her."

Grey shrugged. "Whatever you choose to do with her, it all costs the same. Cash only, of course."

"Go on up, John," said Dead Boy. "I'll have a nice little chat with Grey."

He moved forward, and Grey fell back, because people do when Dead Boy comes walking right at them. Grey quickly recovered himself and put out a hand to

stop Dead Boy. Magic sparkled briefly on the air between them, then sputtered and went out. Grey backed
up against a wall, his eyes very large.

"Who . . . *what* are you?"

"I'm Dead Boy. And that's all you need to know. Get
a move on, John. I don't want to be here all night."

I pulled the door shut behind me, strode past Dead
Boy and Grey, and started up the narrow stairs. Sylvia
was on the next floor. I could feel it. The house was
cold and grim, and the shadows were very dark and
very deep. The stairs were bare wood, without carpeting, but still my feet made hardly any sound as I
climbed. It was like moving through one of those
houses we find in nightmares. Familiar and yet horribly
alien, where every door and every window is a threat,
every sight heavy with terrible significance. Distances
seemed to stretch and contract, and it took forever to
get to the top of the stairs.

There was a door right in front of me. A terrible
door, holding awful secrets behind it. I stood there,
breathing hard, but whether from fear or anticipation I
couldn't tell. It was Sylvia's door. I didn't need to be
told that. I could feel her presence, like the pressure of
a coming storm on the evening air. I pushed the door
with the fingertips of one hand, and it swung smoothly
open before me, inviting me in. I smelled something
that made my nostrils flare, and I walked in.

In the room, in the red room, in the room of rose-
petal light and shifting shadows, it was like walking
into a woman's body. It was warm and humid, and the
still air was heavy with sweat and musk and perfumed
hair. There was no obvious source for the light, but
there were shadows everywhere, as though the delights

the room offered were too subtle to be exposed by bright light. I felt welcomed and desired, and I never wanted to leave.

It was like walking into an antechamber of Hell. And I loved it.

The woman lying at her ease on the oversized bed, naked and smiling and unashamed, was entirely horrible and horribly attractive, like a taste for rotting meat or Russian roulette. She squirmed slowly on the crimson covers like a single maggot in a pool of blood. The details of her face and shape were always moving, changing, shifting subtly from one moment to the next, and even her height and weight were never constant. She could have been one woman or a hundred, or a hundred women in one. Her movements were slow and languorous, and her skin was as white as the white of an eye. Her face was a hundred kinds of beautiful, even when it was unbearably ugly. Her bone structures rose and fell like the turning of the tide, her mouth pursed and widened and changed colour, and her dark, dark eyes promised the kind of pleasures that would make a man cry out in self-disgust as much as passion. I wanted her like I'd never wanted anyone. Her presence filled the room, overpoweringly sexual, awfully female.

And I wanted her the way you always want things you know are bad for you.

"John Taylor," said the woman on the bed. Her voice was soft and caressing, every woman's voice in one. "They thought you might come here. The Cavendishes. I've been so looking forward to having you. They're the ones who made me what I am, even if the result wasn't exactly what they intended. I was just a singer in those days, and a good singer, too, but that wasn't enough for the Cavendishes. They wanted a star who would appeal to absolutely everyone. And this is what they got, this is what their money bought. A woman transformed, a chimera of sex, everything anyone ever desired, and a joy forever."

She laughed, but there was little humour and less humanity in the sound. Her flesh pulsed and shifted in slow rolling movements, never the same twice. My skin crawled, and I couldn't look away to save my life. I had an erection so hard it hurt. Only sheer willpower held me where I was, just inside the doorway. I couldn't go any closer. I didn't dare. I wanted to do things to her, and I wanted her to do things to me.

And then she lazily brought one hand up to her ever-changing mouth. There was something red and sticky on her fingers, and she put it to her mouth and ate it, chewing slowly, savouring the taste. For the first time, as my eyes grew accustomed to the rose-petal light, I realised there was someone else in the room, lying on the floor beside the bed. A man, lying very still, mostly hidden in shadows. A dead man, with his skull caved in. There was a gaping hole in the side of his head, and, as I watched, Sylvia lowered her hand to the hole, dug around in it with her fingers, and pulled out some more brains.

Sylvia's just finished with her last client, Grey had said.

She saw the expression on my face and laughed again. "A girl has to live. There's a price that comes with being what I am, but luckily I'm not the one who has to pay it. They come to me, all the men and the women, drawn to me by desires they didn't even know they had, and I let them sink themselves in my flesh. And while they're busying themselves, I take my toll. I drain them of their desires, their enthusiasms, their faiths and their certainties, and eventually their lives. Though by that stage they usually don't care. And afterwards, I eat them all up. Their vitalities keep me alive, and their flesh helps me maintain my shape. A balance must be struck, between stability and chaos. You wouldn't like what I look like, when I can't get what I need. Oh don't look so shocked, John! The Cavendishes' magic made me all the women you could ever desire, and I love it. Those who come to me know the risks, and *they* love it. This is sex the way it should be, free from all restraints and conscience. Total indulgence, in this best of all possible worlds." She glanced down at the dead body on the floor. "Don't mourn him. He was all used up. No good to himself, or anyone else, except me. And he did die with a smile on his face. See?"

I couldn't speak, couldn't answer her.

She stretched slowly, voluptuous beyond reason. "Don't you want me, John? I can be anyone you ever wanted, and you can do things with me you wouldn't dare do with them. I live for pleasure, and my flesh is very accommodating."

"No." I made myself say it, even though the effort brought beads of sweat out on my face. I learned self-discipline early, just to stay alive. And I was used to not getting what I wanted. But it still took everything I had to stay where I was. "I need . . . to talk to you, Sylvia. About the Cavendishes."

"Oh, I don't think about them any more. I don't care about the outside world. I have made my own little world here, and it is perfect. I never leave it. I glory in it. Have you come here to tell me of the Nightside? Is it still full of sin? How long has it been, since I came here?"

"Just over a year," I said, taking a step forward.

"Is that all? It feels like centuries to me. But then time passes so slowly, in Heaven and Hell."

I took another step forward. Her body called to my body, in a voice as old as the world. I knew it would cost me my life and my soul, and I didn't care. Except some small part of me, screaming deep within me, still *did* care. So I did the only thing I could do, to save myself. I called up my gift, my power, and looked at Sylvia Sin with my third eye, my private eye. I used my gift to find the woman she used to be, before the Cavendishes changed her, and brought her back.

Sylvia screamed, convulsing on the bed, her white flesh boiling and seething, then one shape snapped into focus, one body rising suddenly out of all the others, and the changes stopped. Sylvia lay on the bed, curled up into a ball, breathing hard. One woman, with flesh-coloured flesh and a pretty, ordinary face. I was breathing hard, too, like a man who'd just stepped back from the very brink of a cliff. The overpowering sexual pressure was gone from the room, though faint vestiges of its presence still lingered on the air. Sylvia sat up slowly on the bed, naked and normal, and looked at me with merely human eyes.

"What did you do? *What have you done to me?*"

"I've given you back yourself," I said. "You're free now. Entirely normal."

"I didn't ask to be normal! I liked who I was! What I was! The pleasures and the hungers and the feed-

ing . . . I was a goddess, you bastard! Give it back!
Give it back to me!"

She threw herself at me, launching herself off the
bed like a wildcat, going for my eyes with her hands,
my throat with her teeth. I jumped to one side, and she
missed me, betrayed by her unfamiliar, limited body.
She crashed against the wall by the door, started to
move away and found she couldn't. The wall wouldn't
let her go. Her skin was stuck to the rose-petal surface.
And that was when I realised at last where the rosy
light came from, and why there was still that faint trace
of a presence on the air. You do magical crazy things in
a room long enough, and you get a magical crazy room.
I'd brought Sylvia back, but the room still remained.
She cried out and hit the wall with her fist, and the fist
stuck to the wall. Already she was sinking into it, as
though into a rosy pool, her body being absorbed the
same way she'd engulfed so many others. She didn't
even have time to work up a proper scream before she
was gone, and the sexual presence was suddenly that
much stronger, like the eyes of a hungry predator suddenly turning in my direction.

I ran out of the room, and all the way back down the
stairs.

I stopped at the foot of the stairs and concentrated on
slowing my breathing. My heart was pounding like a
hammer in my chest. There's always temptation in the
Nightside, and one of the first lessons you learn is that
when you've got away, you don't ever look back.
Sylvia Sin was gone, and the room should starve to
death soon enough. As long as some poor damned fool

didn't start feeding it . . . I looked around for Grey. He was crouching huddled in a corner, shaking and shuddering and crying his eyes out. I looked at Dead Boy, leaning casually against the front door.

"What happened to him?" I said.

"He wanted to know what it was like, being dead," said Dead Boy. "So I told him."

I looked at Grey and shuddered. His eyes were very wide and utterly empty.

"So," said Dead Boy. "All finished with Sylvia, are you?"

"She's finished," I said. "The Cavendishes did something to her. Made her a monster. Maybe they've done something to Rossignol, too. I have to go see her again."

"Mind if I tag along?" said Dead Boy. "At least around you death's never boring."

"Sure," I said. "Just let me do all the talking, okay?"

EIGHT

Divas!

Like most cities, there's never anywhere to park in the Nightside when you need it. There are high- and low-rise tesseract car parks and protected areas, but they're never anywhere useful. And cars left unattended on Nightside streets tend to be suddenly stolen, or eaten, or even evolve into something else entirely while your back's turned. But Dead Boy pulled his car of the future in to the curb, just down the street from Caliban's Cavern, got out, and walked away without even a backward glance. I went with him, but couldn't help looking back uncertainly. The shining silver car looked distinctly out of place in the steaming sleazy streets of Uptown. Already certain eyes were studying it with thoughtful intent.

"It will take more than automatic locks to protect your car here," I pointed out.

"My car can take care of itself," Dead Boy said easily. "The onboard computers have access to all kinds of defensive weaponry, together with an exceedingly nasty sense of humour and no conscience at all."

We strolled up the rain-slick street, and the crowds parted in front of us to let us pass. The blazing neon was as sharp and sleazy as ever, and hot saxophone music and heavy bass beats drifted out of the clubs we passed. A small group were sacrificing a street mime to some lesser god, while tourists clustered round with camcorders. A teddy bear with his eyes and mouth sewn shut was handing out flyers protesting animal experimentation. Cooking smells from a dozen different cultures wafted across the still night air. And more than one person saw Dead Boy coming and chose to walk in another direction entirely.

We finally stopped and studied Caliban's Cavern from a discreet distance. The exterior of the nightclub had been thoroughly trashed during the riot, and a team of specialist restorers were on the scene, clearing up the mess and making good with style and speed and uncanny precision. The Nightside has always had a tendency to mayhem and mass destruction, so there's never any shortage of firms ready and willing to undertake quick repairs and restoration, for the usual exorbitant prices. Most of the big concerns were still busy dealing with the chaos and devastation left behind after the recent Angel War, but it seemed the Cavendishes had been able to raise enough cash-in-hand to get some firm on the job straight away. Three builder magicians were using unification spells to put the facia back together. It was quite fun watching the broken and shattered pieces leaping up from the pavement to fit themselves neatly together again like a complex jigsaw. Some other poor sod had the unenviable task of putting the front door back on its hinges, while the simulacrum in the wood cursed him steadily as an unfeeling incompetent, in between lengthy crying jags.

A crowd had gathered to watch, Nightsiders always being interested in free entertainment, and other people had arrived to sell the crowd things it didn't need, like T-shirts, free passes to clubs no-one in their right mind would visit anyway, and various forms of hot food. This usually consisted of something nasty and overpriced in a bun, that only the most newly arrived tourists would be dumb enough actually to eat.

Dead Boy sniffed loudly as some fool in a grubby dressing gown handed over good money in return for something allegedly meat-based in a tortilla. "Proof if proof were needed," he said loudly, "that tourists will eat absolutely anything. Truth in advertising, that's what's needed here. See how well that stuff would sell if the vendors were obliged to shout the truth. *Something wriggling on a stick! Pies containing creatures whose name you couldn't even spell! Food so fast it will be out your backside before you know it!*"

"Buyer beware," I said easily. "That should be the Nightside's motto. Nothing's ever what it seems . . ."

We watched interestedly as one of the builder magicians used a temporal reverse spell to restore some damaged woodwork, then joined in the general jeering as he let the spell get away from him, and time sped back too far, so that the wood started sprouting branches and leaves again. Dead Boy looked the night-club over with his professionally deceased eyes.

"There are new and really nasty magical wards all over the place," he said quietly. "They're well disguised, but there's not much you can hide from the dead. It's mostly shaped curses and proximity hexes, an awful lot of them keyed specifically to your presence, John. We're only just out of range here. The Cavendishes really don't want you anywhere near their club again."

"How nasty are we talking?" I said.

"Put it this way—if you were to trigger even one of these quite appalling little bear-traps, they'll be scraping your remains off the surroundings with a palette knife."

"Ouch," I said. "I still have to get in to see Rossignol. Any ideas?"

Dead Boy considered the matter. People saw him frowning and moved even further away, just in case. "I could walk in," he said finally. "Those defences are only dangerous to the living."

"No," I said. "First, Rossignol wouldn't talk to you, only me. And second, you'd be bound to set off all kinds of alarms. I really don't want to attract the Cavendishes' attention if I can help it. They've got a Power on their side. The Jonah."

"Ah yes, young Billy. Nasty piece of work. If he ever grew a pair, he could be really dangerous."

"The odds are, Rossignol is still in her room over the club, guarded by a couple of heavy-duty combat magicians. I bluffed them once, but twice would definitely be pushing it. And who knows what other surprises they've got set up in there . . ."

"So what do you want to do, John?" said Dead Boy, just a little impatiently. "We can't just stand around out there. Word will get around. How are we going to get to your deadly little songbird? Come on, think devious. It's what you do best."

"If we can't get in to her," I said slowly, "she'll have to come out to us. We'll send her a message. Most of the club's staff will be kicking their heels somewhere close at hand, keeping out of the way and waiting for the repairs to be finished. All we have to do is track them down and find someone we can bribe, convince, or intimidate into passing Rossignol our message."

"They could be anywhere," Dead Boy said doubtfully. "What are you going to do, use your gift to locate them?"

"No," I said. "I don't think so. I've been using my gift too much, too often, lately. And every time I open up my mind, my thoughts blaze like a beacon in the night. My enemies can use that to find me. And you know some of the things they've sent after me. No, I've pushed my luck as far as I dare. It's time to be sensible and stick to simple deduction. All we have to do is check out the local bars, cafes, and diners, and we'll find the club. Theatricals never can go for long without their creature comforts."

We found them all just a short walk further up the street, at the Honey Bee, an overly lit but very clean theme coffee bar, where all the waitresses were obliged to wear puffy black-and-yellow-striped bee outfits, together with bobbly antennae and spiked heel stilettos. They didn't look too happy about it as they tottered unsteadily between the tables, reeling off the specials through practiced smiles. The chorus girls from Caliban's Cavern had wedged themsleves into a corner, nursing their cups of distressed coffee, chattering loudly and smoking up a storm. Also present was one Ian Auger, roadie and musician, and the only one who seemed at all pleased to see me as Dead Boy and I approached their table.

"Oh it's you again, is it?" said the platinum blonde backing singer, flicking her ash disdainfully onto the floor. "Trouble on legs and twice as unfortunate. Everything was fine until you turned up. Then you show your face, and we get a suicide in the front row and a riot in the house. The Authorities should ban you, on general principles."

"It's been tried," I said calmly. "And I'm still here. I need someone to take a message to Rossignol." I looked around, hoping for a sympathetic smile, but it was all glowering faces and curled lips. I couldn't really blame them. One of the problems of having a carefully cultivated bad reputation like mine is that I tend to get the blame for everything that goes wrong around me.

"Who's your pale friend with no fashion sense?" said the blonde.

"This is Dead Boy," I said, and the whole coffee-house went suddenly quiet. Ian Auger pushed back his chair and stood up.

"Let's talk outside," he said resignedly. "You mustn't mind the girls. They're never keen on anything that might put their jobs at risk." We moved over to stand in the doorway, while the other customers and staff studied us warily. Ian Auger looked at me, frowning. "I'm worried about Ross. The Cavendishes have been all over her since the suicide, telling her what to do, what to say, what to think. All they seem to care about is what spin they can put on the suicide for the music media. Ross is practically a prisoner at the moment, under armed guard. Are you still interested in helping her?"

"Of course," I said. "Can you get a message to her?"

"Maybe," said Ian. "At least, one of me might be able to."

"Which one of them are you?" I said.

"All of them," Ian Auger said cheerfully. "I'm a temporal triplet. One soul, three bodies, no waiting. Close-part harmonies a speciality. Me mum always said Destiny stuttered when I was born. Right now my other two selves are busy inside the club, putting the stage set back together again. They're listening to you through me. What's the message?"

"Nothing good," I said. "The Cavendishes tried to make one of their singers into a superstar before. They had a young girl called Sylvia Sin magically augmented, to make her even more popular, and it turned her into a monster. Quite literally. I've seen what they did to her, what she became, and I don't want anything like that to happen to Ross. I need her to sneak out of the club and join me somewhere safe, so we can work out what to do for the best. I don't trust the Cavendishes to have her best interests at heart. It shouldn't be too difficult for Ross to get out. Bodyguards are usually more interested in watching for people trying to sneak in."

Ian scowled fiercely. "Sylvia Sin. There's a name I haven't thought of in a while. Always wondered what happened to her. All right, one of me will talk to Ross. She might listen, now the Cavendishes have left the club. She always seems brighter and more independent when they're not around."

"They do seem to have an unhealthy hold over her," I said. "Could they already have done something to her?"

"I don't know," said Ian. "No-one's allowed to get too close when the Cavendishes are in private conference with Ross. And there's no denying she's not been acting like herself since she came to live in that room over the club. You think if the Cavendishes have done something, that's what's causing the suicides?"

"Could be," I said.

"All right," said Ian. "If I can get a message to her, and if I can get her out of the club, where do you want to meet? It has to be somewhere secure, somewhere she can feel safe, and somewhere she won't be noticed. She has got a pretty famous face now, you know."

"I know the perfect place to hide a famous face," said Dead Boy. "Hide her in a whole crowd of famous faces. Tell Rossignol to meet us at Divas!"

Divas! is one of the more famous, or possibly infamous, nightclubs in Uptown, where you can go to see and hear all the most famous female singers in the history of entertainment. Of course, none of them are real. They're not even female. The famous faces are in fact transvestites, men dressed up as the women they adore. But dressed in style and made up to the nines, the illusion is more than perfect, for these trannies have taken their obsession one step further than most—they have learned to channel the talents and sometimes the personalities of the divas concerned. Dead or alive, the greatest stars of show business all come to Divas!, in proxy at least.

Dead Boy had clearly been there before. The doorman held the door to the club open and bowed very low, and no-one asked us if we were members, or even to pay the cover charge. The hatcheck girl was a 1960s Cilla Black in a black bustier, and from the wink she dropped Dead Boy it was clear he was a regular. Cilla did her best to ignore me, but I'm used to that. Dead Boy is one of the Nightside's celebrities. I'm more of an anti-celebrity. We made our way into the club itself, which was all silks and flowers and bright colours. The furniture was all art deco, and everywhere you looked was every kind of kitsh fashion you ever shuddered at in disbelief. Chandeliers and disco balls hung side by side from the ceiling.

The main floor was crowded, and the noise level was appalling. The night is always jumping at Divas! Dead Boy and I edged between the tightly packed tables, following a waitress. All the waitresses were channeling Liza Minnelli tonight, dressed in her *Cabaret* outfit. We ended up at a table tucked away in a corner and ordered over-priced drinks from the Liza. I asked for a glass of Coke, and then had to go through my usual routine of *No, I don't want a Diet Coke! I want a real Coke! A man's Coke! And I don't want a bloody straw either!* Dead Boy ordered a bottle of gin and the best cigar they had. I made a note of the prices for my expenses sheet. You have to keep track of things like that, or you can go broke on some cases.

"What if Rossignol doesn't turn up?" said Dead

Boy, raising his voice to be heard over the general clamour. "What if she can't get away?"

"Then we'll think of something else," I said. "Relax. Enjoy the show. It's costing us enough."

"What do you mean *us*, white man?"

Up on the stage at the far end of the room, an Elaine and a Barbara were dueting on a pretty accurate rendition of "I Know Him So Well." The channelling must be going well tonight. Other famous faces paraded across the floor of the club, there to see and be seen, stopping at tables to chat and gossip and show themselves off. Marilyn and Dolly, Barbra and Dusty. Elaine and Barbara were replaced on stage by a Nico, who favoured us with her mournful voice and presence as she husked "It Took More Than One Man to Change My Name to Shanghai Lily" into the microphone, accompanying herself on the accordion. I just hoped she wouldn't do the Doors's "The End." There's only so much existential angst I can take before my ears start bleeding.

A few tables away, two Judys were having a vicious wig-pulling fight. Spectators cheered them on and laid bets.

And then Ian Auger came in, with Rossignol on his arm, and no-one in Divas! paid her any attention, because everyone assumed she was another trannie, perhaps a little more convincing than some. Ian escorted her over to our table, pulled out her chair for her, introduced her to Dead Boy, and politely but firmly refused to sit down himself.

"I can't hang about here. I've got to get back. There's still a lot of work to do in the club, and I don't want to be missed."

"Any trouble getting Ross here?" I asked.

"Surprisingly, no. I just told the bodyguards that John Taylor was somewhere on the loose in the building, and they all went running off to look for you. We strolled right out. Look, I really do have to go. Ross, remember you're due to go on again in just under an hour."

Rossignol let him kiss her on the cheek, and he hurried away, his hunchback giving him a weird rolling gait. The waitress Liza came back to take Rossignol's order. I looked Rossignol over as she studied the wine list. She looked different. Same pale face, dark hair, little black dress. But she seemed somehow sharper, brighter, more focussed. She looked up, caught me watching, and smiled broadly.

"Ah, John, it is so good to be out and about for a change. You know what I want? I want five whiskey sours. I want them all at once, all lined up in front of me so I can look at them while I'm drinking them. I'm never allowed to drink in Caliban's Cavern, by order of the Cavendishes, though strangely, mostly I don't want to. I stick to the healthy diet they provide, and I never complain, both of which are also very unlike me. Cake! I want cake! Bring me the biggest, gooiest chocolate gateau you have, and a big spoon! I want everything that's bad for me, and I want it right now!"

The waitress whooped with glee. "You go, girl!"

I indicated for the waitress to bring Rossignol what she wanted, and the Liza tottered away on her high heels. Rossignol beamed happily.

"The Cavendishes are always very strict about what I'm allowed to have, and do. They act more like my mother than my managers."

"I notice they didn't stop you smoking," I said.

She snorted loudly. "I'd like to see them try." She stopped smiling suddenly and gave me a hard look. "Ian tells me that you've been out and about on my behalf, speaking to people. And that you found out something concerning my predecessor with the Cavendishes. I remember her face being on all the magazine covers, then . . . nothing. What did happen to her, John? What did the Cavendishes do to her?"

I told her enough of the story to scare her, without dwelling on some of the nastier details. Dead Boy shot me the occasional glance as he realised what I was doing, but he kept his peace. He'd already drunk half his bottle of gin and had started eating his cigar. When I finally finished, Ross let out a long sigh.

"I had no idea. The poor thing. And the Cavendishes did that to her?"

"More likely had it done," I said. "Have they ever offered to . . . do anything for you?"

"No. Never." Rossignol's voice was firm and sharp. "I'd have told them where they could stick their magic. I don't need any of that shit to be a success. I'm a singer, and all I've ever needed are my songs and my voice." And then she stopped and frowned suddenly. "And yet, having said that . . . things have changed since I came to live in my little room over the club. My songs are always sad songs now. And there are some odd gaps in my memory. I feel cold, and tired, all of the time. And the way I act when the Cavendishes are around . . . doesn't feel like me at all. Could they have worked a magic on me, without my knowing?"

"It's possible," I said carefully. "They could have done something, then made you forget it. The

Cavendishes don't strike me as being particularly burdened with professional ethics."

The waitress arrived with the five whiskey sours on a tray. Rossignol cooed happily as they were lined up in front of her, then knocked back the first two, one after the other. She breathed heavily for a moment, then giggled happily, like a small child who's just done something naughty and doesn't give a damn. "Yes! Oh yes! That hit the spot!" She smiled charmingly at me, then at Dead Boy. "So, what's it like, being dead?"

"Don't tell her!" I said sharply, then looked apologetically at the startled singer. "Sorry about that, but some questions are best left unanswered. Especially when it concerns him."

"Like why he's eating that cigar instead of smoking it?"

"Very probably."

She smiled at me again, a warm and embracing moment quite at odds with her earlier, somewhat distanced personality. "You've been known to avoid answering questions yourself on occasion, *monsieur* mystery man." Her French accent had become slightly more pronounced after the third whiskey sour. I couldn't get over how alive she seemed. She looked at me thoughtfully. "You don't really think the Cavendishes would do anything to harm me, do you? I mean, they're relying on me to make them a great deal of money."

"Maybe they thought they were helping Sylvia," I said. "But there's the suicides, Ross. The Cavendishes have to be connected to that somehow. I don't trust them, and you shouldn't either. You say the word, and Dead Boy and I will take you away from them right now. We'll find you somewhere safe to lie low while we get some lawyers in to check out your contract, and maybe a few experts to make sure you haven't been messed about with magically. You don't have to worry. I can guarantee your safety. I know any number of people who'd be only too happy to bodyguard you. Not very nice people, perhaps, but . . ."

"No," said Rossignol, kindly but firmly. "It's a very generous offer, John, and I do appreciate you're only trying to help, but . . ."

"But?"

"But this is my big break. My chance to be a star. No-one has connections like the Cavendishes. They really can get me a contract with a major recording studio. I have to do this. I have to sing. It's all I've ever wanted, all I've ever cared about. I can't back out now. I won't back out over what could be just a case of nerves. You don't have any proof they've done anything wrong, do you?"

"No," I said. "But the suicides . . ."

She grimaced. "Trust me, I haven't forgotten. I'll never forget the look on that poor man's face as he pulled the trigger right in front of me. He looked right into my eyes, and he was smiling . . . I can't let that go on. My singing was always supposed to make people feel good! I wanted to lift their hearts and comfort them, send them back out to face the world feeling renewed . . . If the Cavendishes really have done something to corrupt my songs, my voice . . ." She shook her head sharply. "Oh, I don't know! I don't know what to do!" She picked up the fourth whiskey sour and stared at it moodily.

We all sat and considered the matter for a while. Up

on the stage, a Whitney was singing "I Will Always Love You." Rossignol sniffed loudly.

"Never cared for that. Far too strident."

"I prefer the Dolly Parton version," said Dead Boy, unexpectedly. "More warmth."

I looked at him. "You're just full of surprises, aren't you?"

"You have no idea," said Dead Boy.

Rossignol put the fourth whiskey sour to one side as the chocolate gateau arrived. It really was very big, with scrapings of dark and white chocolate sprinkled on the top. Rossignol made ooh- and aah-ing noises, and her eyes went very wide. She grabbed the spoon and stuck it in, and soon there were chocolate smears all round her mouth. I considered her thoughtfully. An unpleasant idea had suggested itself. Perhaps the reason why this Rossignol seemed so different from the one I'd encountered at Caliban's Cavern, was because this was an entirely different Rossignol. Another duplicate, like the tulpa who'd wrecked the *Night Times*'s offices. It would explain a lot, including how she'd been able to get out of the club so easily.

"I think I need to go to the little boy's room," I said loudly, giving Dead Boy a meaningful look.

"Fine," he said. "Thanks for sharing that with us, John."

"This is the first time I've been to this club," I said pointedly. "Why don't you show me where the Gents is?"

"I've never had to use it," said Dead Boy. "One of the few advantages of being dead."

I glared at him and made furious eyebrow gestures while Rossignol was busy making ecstatic chocolate-

eating noises, and he finally got the point. We got to
our feet, excused ourselves, and headed for the nearby
door marked *Stand Up*. Once inside, the shiny-tiled ex-
panse was empty apart from a Kylie standing at the uri-
nal with his skirt hiked up. Dead Boy and I waited until
he'd finished, taking a keen interest in the vending machines, and once the Kylie was gone, Dead Boy gave
me a hard look.

"This had better be important, John. Just being in
here alone with you is undoubtedly doing my reputation no good at all."

"Shut up and listen. The Cavendishes have already
sent one duplicate Rossignol after me—a tulpa with
supernatural strength and a really bad attitude. Is there
any way you can tell whether that's the real Rossignol
or not? You're always saying nothing can be hidden
from the dead."

"Oh sure. I've already checked her out."

"And?"

"She is the original. And she's dead."

I looked at him for a long moment. "She's *what?*"

"She doesn't have an aura. It was the first thing I noticed about her."

"Well, why didn't you say anything?"

"It's none of my business if she's mortally challenged. You need to be more open-minded, John."

"You mean, she's dead, like you?"

"Oh no. I'm a special case. And she's far too bright
and bubbly to be a zombie. But you can't be alive without an aura. Everyone has one."

"Really?" I said, momentarily distracted. "What
does mine look like?"

"Lots of purple."

"How can she be dead and not know it?" I said, almost as angry as I was exasperated. "She's out there right now giving every indication of being very much alive. Dead people don't have orgasms over chocolate gateau."

"Denial isn't just a river in Egypt. Or perhaps it's something to do with the Cavendishes and their hold over her. Do you want me to break the news to her?"

"No, I think it should come from someone who's at least heard of tact. And she did say she wanted the truth, whatever it was." I scowled at the immaculately shining white tiles. "How do you tell someone they're dead?"

"With your mouth. After all, it could be worse."

"How?"

Dead Boy gave me one of his looks. "Trust me, John. You really don't want to know."

"Oh shut up."

By the time we got back to our table, Rossignol had demolished fully half of the gateau and drunk the other two whiskey sours. She waved happily at us the moment we reappeared and stopped to suck the chocolate smears off her fingers. Her face was flushed, and she kept lapsing into fits of the giggles. Dead Boy and I sat down facing her.

"I want more drinks!" she said cheerfully. "Everybody should have lots more drinks! Do you want some cake? I can ask them for another spoon. No? You don't know what you're missing. Some days, chocolate is better than sex! Well, some sex, anyway. What are you both looking so dour for? Did you find your phone number on a wall in there?"

I took a deep breath and told Rossignol what Dead Boy had discovered about her, and what it meant. I said it as simply and straightforwardly as I could, and then I sat there, waiting to see how she'd take it. All the bounce went out of her, but her face was set and calm. Her gaze was far away and thoughtful, as she slowly licked chocolate off the back of her spoon. She might have been considering a business proposition, or the loss of a distant relative. When she finally looked at me, her gaze was entirely steady, and when she spoke, her voice seemed more resigned than anything else.

"It would explain a lot," she said. "The gaps in my memory, why I'm always so cold, why I'm always so docile when the Cavendishes are around. They did this to me. The old me, the true me, would never have put up with the way they've been treating me. Being here, away from them, is like waking up from some dark, listless nightmare. Only I'm not going to wake up from this dream, am I? I'm dead."

I wanted to take her in my arms and comfort her, tell her everything was going to be all right, but I'd promised her I'd never lie to her. She worried her lower lip between her teeth for a while, then she looked from me to Dead Boy and back again.

"Is there anything you can do to help me? Or at least find out what these cochons did to me?"

"I can try," said Dead Boy, surprisingly gently. "I have learned to See all kinds of things that are hidden from the living. It helps that you and I are both dead. It gives me a link I can use." He took her hand in his and gestured for me to take his other hand. I did so, a little hesitantly. I still remembered what he'd done to Grey. Dead Boy smiled briefly. "Don't wet yourself, John. I'm just going to look into Rossignol's mind and call up a vision of her last moments alive. Her memory is probably blocked by the trauma of what happened. As long as both of you are linked to me, you'll be able to see what I See. But remember, it's just a vision of the past. We can't interfere or intervene. The past cannot be changed, no matter how much we might wish to."

His grip tightened on my hand, and suddenly we were somewhere else. No incantations, no objects of power—just the will of a man who'd been dead for thirty years and still wouldn't lie down. We were in the Cavendishes' inner office, the place to which I had been dragged, broken and bleeding. Mr. and Mrs. Cavendish were smiling at a preoccupied and scowling Rossignol. She was trying to tell them something, but they weren't listening. Mrs. Cavendish poured Rossignol a glass of champagne and said something soothing. Rossignol snatched the glass out of her hand, knocked it back in one, and threw the glass aside. Then she fell heavily to the floor, as her legs betrayed her. She lay there, convulsing and frothing at the mouth, while Mr. and Mrs. Cavendish looked on, smiling. Until, finally, she lay still. Then the Cavendishes looked at someone standing in the shadows, but I couldn't make out who the third person was.

We were suddenly back at our table again. Dead Boy had let go of our hands. Rossignol was trembling, but her mouth was a firm, flat line. She made herself be still with an effort of will.

"The Cavendishes poisoned me?" said Rossignol. "Why would they want to murder their meal ticket?"

"A good question," I said. "And one I think we should ask them, in a pointed and forcible manner."

"You could also ask them what they did to her afterwards," said Dead Boy. He looked at Rossignol speculatively. "You don't act like any kind of zombie I'm familiar with. You're quite definitely deceased, but there are still traces of life about you."

"Could the Cavendishes have made a deal like yours?" I said. "Presumably on her behalf, as her management."

"No," Dead Boy said firmly. "Such compacts can only be entered into willingly. That's the point. You can't just lose your soul—you have to sell it."

"Still," I said, "any kind of magic that can raise the dead is by definition the work of a major player. There was someone else in that office, even if we couldn't make out who it was. The only Power the Cavendishes have on their side that I know of is the Jonah. And while he may become a Power and a Domination eventually, like his father, he's no necromancer."

"How does any of this tie in to the people killing themselves after they've heard me sing?" said Rossignol. Her face was still calm and controlled, but her voice was becoming increasingly brittle.

"You went into the dark," said Dead Boy. "And when you came back, you brought some of it with you. It comes out in your songs, when you sing. That's what's killing people."

"*How could they?*" said Rossignol. "How could the Cavendishes do something like that? My songs were always about life and being positive, even when I wrote about sad things. My voice was meant to raise people up, not destroy them! The Cavendishes have ruined the one thing that gave my life meaning!" Her voice threatened to crack then, but still she held on with iron self-control. Her hands were clenched into fists on top of the table. "I won't let this go on. No more people dead because of me. I want my old voice back. I want my life back!" She glared at Dead Boy, then at me. "Can you help me? Either of you?"

"I can't even help myself," Dead Boy said quietly.

"Let's not give up all hope just yet," I said quickly. "Dead Boy, you said yourself she's not like any other revenant you've ever met. Let's find out exactly what was done to her. Some magical deaths can be reversed."

"You think the Cavendishes will agree to that?" said Dead Boy.

"I don't plan to give them any choice," I said, and my voice was so cold that even Dead Boy had to look away.

And that was when a wave of quiet swept across the club. The music and the singing cut off abruptly in mid number, and the chatter from the surrounding tables died swiftly away to nothing. We all looked around and found every diva in the place staring straight at us. Every trannie, every celebrity by proxy, was up on their feet and staring at us with dark, malignant eyes. Their painted faces were suddenly strange, twisted, shaped by new and deadly emotions. It was like being suddenly surrounded by a pack of wolves. Rossignol and Dead Boy and I rose slowly to our feet, and a frisson of anticipation moved through the menacing crowd. They all smiled at the same moment, a grimace that was all teeth and no humour. One of the Marilyns produced a knife from out of his puffed sleeve. As though that was a signal, dozens of other divas suddenly had weapons in their hands, everything from knives to razor blades to the occasional derringer. Several of them smashed bottles and glasses against tables to make jagged-edged weapons.

"They've been possessed," Dead Boy said quietly. "I know the signs. Their auras have changed. They were channelling the talents and even some of the personalities of their heroines, but that channel has been overridden by a stronger signal, imposed from outside. There's something new and a whole lot nastier in those bodies now."

"Could it be The Primal?" I said. "Back for another crack at us?"

"No," said Dead Boy. "The signs are still human."

A Dusty lurched suddenly forward to stare at Rossignol with unblinking eyes. "We are your greatest fans. We worship you. We adore you. We would die for you. You shouldn't be here. We have come to take you back where you belong."

"Bloody hell," I said. "It's that bunch of Goths and geeks the Cavendishes let hang around their outer office. The fan club from Hell. The Cavendishes must have put them in the divas' heads and sent them to bring Ross back."

"You can't stay here," the Dusty said to Rossignol, ignoring me. "These people are no good for you. You must come with us, back to the Cavendishes. They will make you the star you were born to be. Come with us, now."

"And if she doesn't?" I said.

Without any change of expression, the Dusty slashed at my throat with his knife. I jerked my head back, and he only just missed. The other divas surged forward, raising the weapons in their hands. All the Judys, Kylies, Marilyns, Nicos, and Blondies. Famous faces, marred and twisted by second-hand rage and envy. Someone was threatening to take their goddess away from them, and they would die or kill to prevent that. In their minds, they were rescuing their heroine. Dusty cut at me again. I caught his wrist, twisted it till the fingers reluctantly opened, dropping the knife, then I punched him out. Dead Boy was picking divas up and throwing them around like rag dolls. But there were always more, pressing remorselessly closer, some with improvised weapons like spiked stiletto heels, long hairpins, and clawed fingernails. A Kate Bush came at me shrieking, with a long dagger in his hand. I grabbed Dead Boy and pulled him between us, using his dead body as a shield. The knife slammed into his chest up to the hilt.

"You bastard, Taylor!" said Dead Boy, and then rather spoiled the effect by giggling. I heaved his dead body this way and that, deflecting attacks. It soaked up the punishment, and Dead Boy didn't object. I think he was getting a weird kind of kick out of it. Rossignol was beside me, fighting dirty, pulling trannies' wigs down over their eyes and kicking them in the nuts when she could get a clear target. My back slammed up against the wall behind me, and I yelled past Dead Boy's shoulder for Rossignol to overturn our table and make it a barricade. She broke away from shoulder-charging a Nico and pulled the table over, and soon all three of us were sheltering behind it.

"I'm bored with this," said Dead Boy. "I know a curse that will boil their brains in their heads."

"No!" I said quickly. "We can't kill any of them! The divas aren't responsible for this. They're the victims here."

"Oh hell," said Dead Boy. "It's good deeds time again, is it?"

The divas, all of them eerily silent, swarmed around us, trying to reach us with their weapons and clawed hands. We were safe for the moment, but we were trapped in our corner. There was nowhere left for us to go, and soon enough the divas would work together to pull the table away; and then . . . I swore regretfully, and reluctantly did what I do best. I concentrated and opened up my inner eye, my third eye, and used my gift to find the channel the fans were using to drive the divas. It was like suddenly seeing a shimmering latticework of silver strings, rising up from the divas' heads and sailing off into infinity. And having seen it, it was the easiest thing in the world to locate the single thread they all connected to, the focus for the overlaying signal. It turned out to be a single diva, a Whitney, standing watching from the stage. All I had to do was point the Whitney out to Dead Boy, and he made a swift crushing motion with his fist. The Whitney crumpled unconscious to the stage, and all of the silver lines snapped off.

The spell was broken in a moment, and the attacking divas were suddenly nothing more than disoriented men in frocks and make-up. They stopped where they were, shocked and confused, some clinging to each other for mutual support and comfort. Possession is a kind of violation, of the mind and the soul. For a moment, it actually seemed the danger was over. I should have known better.

The trannies suddenly screamed and scattered as a dozen dark and dangerous figures appeared out of nowhere. Tall menacing figures, with smart suits and no faces. I had used my gift once too often, burned too brightly in the night, and now my enemies had found me again. They had sent the Harrowing for me. The trannies quickly cleared the floor and disappeared out the exits. It had all been too much for them. I would have run, too, if I could. The Harrowing advanced slowly towards us, unstoppable figures of death and horror. They had human shapes, but they didn't move like people did, and the faces under their wide-brimmed hats were only stretches of blank skin. They had no eyes, but they could see. One of them raised its hand, showing me the hypodermic needles where its fingernails should have been. Thick green drops pulsed from the tips of the needles, and I shuddered. Rossignol was clutching my arm so hard it hurt. Dead Boy was frowning for the first time.

"Would I be right in thinking events have just taken a distinct turn for the worse?"

"Oh yes," I said. "They're the Harrowing. The hounds my enemies send after me. You can't hurt or kill them because they're not real. Just constructs. And there's nothing you or I can do to stop them."

"How do you normally deal with them?" said Rossignol.

"I run like hell. I've spent a lot of my life running from the Harrowing." I raised my gift again, desperately trying to find a way out, but there wasn't one. There was no exit close enough to reach, and the over-turned table wouldn't slow them down for a second. The dozen vicious figures moved towards us, relentless as cancer, implacable as destiny. And then a female figure came howling out of nowhere and launched itself at one of the Harrowing. The attacker had been a Kylie once, but all traces of glamour and femininity had been torn away by recent traumas. All that mattered to the Kylie now was that there was a target for his rage. He stabbed the Harrowing in the chest, and its pliant body just absorbed the blow, taking no damage and trapping both the knife and the hand inside its unnatural flesh. The Harrowing made a brief slashing gesture with one hand, and the Kylie just fell apart into a hundred pieces, blood spurting and gushing all over the floor.

"Damn," said Dead Boy. "That is seriously nasty. You know, I have to wonder . . . how many pieces could you cut me into, and I'd still be able to put myself back together again?"

"Well, unless you fancy life as a jigsaw, stop wondering about it and bloody well do something," I said, stridently.

"Boys," said Rossignol. "They really are getting terribly close. Please tell me one of you has something resembling a plan."

"When you get right down to it," said Dead Boy, "I'm just a walking corpse who's picked up a few unpleasant strategems along the way. There's nothing in my bag of tricks that could even slow those bastards down. You have really powerful enemies, John."

"Okay," I said, my mouth almost painfully dry. "That's it. Dead Boy, grab Ross and run like hell. As long as you're not a threat, they might not bother with you. They're only here for me."

"What will they do to you?" said Rossignol.

"If I'm lucky, they'll kill me quickly," I said. "But

I've never been that lucky. The Harrowing are horror and despair. Please, get out of here."

"I can't leave you," said Dead Boy. "Good deeds, remember? Abandoning you now would set me back years."

"And I won't leave you," said Rossignol. "If only because you're my only hope of breaking free from the Cavendishes."

"Please," I said. "You don't understand. If you stay, they'll do . . . horrible things to you. I've seen it happen before."

"You'll think of something, John," said Rossignol. "I know you will."

But I didn't. I'd never been able to face the Harrowing, only run from them. My very own pursuing demons. The first of the Harrowing grabbed one edge of our barricading table with a puffy corpse-pale hand and threw it aside as though it were nothing. Dead Boy braced himself, and I pushed Rossignol behind me, sheltering her with my body. And then all the Harrowing stopped and turned their featureless faces, as though listening to something only they could hear. They started to shake and shudder, and then one by one they fell apart into rot and slime, slumping shapelessly to the floor. One moment a dozen menacing figures were closing in on us, and the next there was nothing but thick puddles of reeking ooze, spreading slowly. Dead Boy and I looked at each other, and then we both glared round sharply at the sound of soft, mocking laughter. And there, standing on the stage at the end of the room was Billy Lathem, the Jonah, in his smart, smart suit. He looked very pleased with himself. Stand-

ing on either side of him in their undertakers' clothes
were Mr. and Mrs. Cavendish.

"I told you, John," said the Jonah. "I am far more
powerful than you ever realised. I am entropy, the end
of all things, and not even sendings like those ugly bastards can stand against me. Now, you have something
that doesn't belong to you. And I have come to repos-
sess it."

"Come along, dear Rossignol," said Mr. Cavendish.
"You'll be late for your show."

"You don't want to be late for your show, do you?"
said Mrs. Cavendish.

Rossignol was still gripping my arm tightly. "I won't
go with them. Don't let them take me, John. I can't go
back to being the half-asleep thing I was, nodding and
smiling and agreeing to everything they said. I'd rather
die."

"You don't have to go anywhere you don't want to,"
I said, but it didn't sound convincing, even to me. I was
still stunned at how easily the Jonah had destroyed the
Harrowing. He *had* become a Power and a Domination,
like his late father, Count Entropy, and I was just a man
with a gift. And a bad reputation . . . I raised my head
and gave Billy Lathem one of my best enigmatic looks.

"We've done this dance before, Billy. Back off, or
I'll use my gift . . ."

"You don't dare," said the Jonah, grinning nastily.
"Not now your enemies know where you are. What do
you think they'll send next, if you're dumb enough to
open up your mind again? Something so appalling even
I might not be able to deal with it. No, your only option
now is to hand over the girl and skulk off out of here,
before your enemies track you down anyway." He

laughed suddenly. "You'll never be able to bluff anyone ever again, John. Not after I tell everyone how I saw you cringing and helpless, and hiding behind a table. And all from things I turned to rot and slime with just a wave of my hand. Now, you back off, John. Or I'll use my power to find the one piece of bad luck that will break you forever."

NINE

Seeing the Light, at Last

And so, one of the messiest and most messed-up cases of my career came to this—showdown at the Divas! saloon. The only trouble was, in the Jonah the Cavendishes had by far the biggest gun. His reducing of the Harrowing to so much multi-coloured mush had been truly impressive. Never thought the boy had it in him. Perhaps staring him down and humiliating him in front of his employers hadn't been such a great idea after all. Certainly something had put a rocket up his arse. You could practically see his power crackling on the air around him, writhing and coiling, bad luck waiting to be born and cursed on the living.

We stood there in our two groups, at opposite ends of the ballroom, separated by a sea of overturned tables and chairs, and the suppurating remains of the Harrowing. Mr. and Mrs. Cavendish in their shabby undertakers' outfits, and the Jonah in his smart, smart suit, standing by the entrance doors. And me, Dead Boy, and Rossignol, standing by our abandoned barricade. The good guys and the bad guys, face to face for the inevitable confrontation.

I was looking unobtrusively around for an exit. I've never been much of a one for this kind of confrontation if there's an exit handy.

"Kill them," said Mr. Cavendish, in his cold, clipped voice.

"Kill them all," said Mrs. Cavendish, in her sharp clear voice.

"No," said the Jonah, and both the Cavendishes looked at him, surprised. He smiled, unmoved. "I want to see them suffer first."

The Cavendishes looked at each other. Both of them started to say something, then stopped. They considered the Jonah thoughtfully. Something had just changed in their relationship with their hired gun, and they weren't sure what.

"Come up onstage, all of you," said Billy Lathem, the Jonah, son of Count Entropy. "I want you to know exactly how badly you've failed, John. I want to explain it all to you, so you can see you never really stood a chance."

"Why should I do anything you say, Billy?" I said, genuinely interested in what his answer would be.

"Because I'll tell you the truth about what we did to poor dear Rossignol," said the Jonah.

Just like that he had me where he wanted me, and we both knew it. So I shrugged casually and headed for the stage, with all my hackles stirring. Something bad was coming, I could feel it, and it was aimed right at me. Dead Boy and Rossignol came with me. The Jonah said a few low words to the Cavendishes, and they followed him up onto the opposite side of the stage. We all stopped a cautious distance apart, then we all looked at the Jonah, to see how he wanted to play this. He was smiling a happy cruel smile, a predator about to play with his prey, for a while.

"We allowed Rossignol to escape from Caliban's Cavern," the Jonah said easily, "in order that we could follow her, to you. We were waiting for someone to make contact with her, and it wasn't really any surprise when the go-between turned out to be the besotted and predictable and stupidly loyal Ian Auger. The Cavendishes wanted me to trail Rossignol, then . . . take care of things, but I persuaded them to come along. I wanted them to see me take you down, John, to watch and appreciate as I destroy you, inch by inch. They don't get out much these days. Well, you can tell that from their awful pallor, can't you? I've seen things crawl out from under rocks sporting better tans. And they really don't like to be out and about in public, but I wanted them to be here, so here they are. Isn't it marvelous how things can work out, if you just put your mind to it?"

"So the servant becomes the master," I observed to the Cavendishes. "Or the monster turns on his creator, if you prefer. Not for the first time, of course. You do remember Sylvia Sin, don't you?"

"Charming girl," said Mr. Cavendish. "Always said she'd go far, didn't I, Mrs. Cavendish?"

"Indeed you did, Mr. Cavendish." The woman

looked at me thoughtfully. "Have you seen the dear girl recently?"

"Yes," I said. "She was a monster. So I put her out of the misery you put her into."

"Oh good," said the woman. "We do so detest loose ends. And as for the Jonah—why, he is our dear friend and ally, and we are very proud of him. We predict great things for him, in the future."

"Couldn't have put it better," said the man. "A person to be watched, and studied."

"What happened to Ian?" Rossignol said suddenly. "What did you do to him?"

"Ah yes," said the Jonah. "Never cared much for the shifty little runt. Let's just say that the trio . . . has now become a duet." He sniggered loudly at his own wit, while Rossignol turned her head away. The Jonah looked at the Cavendishes. "Tell them. Tell them everything. I want them to know it all, to know how badly they've failed, before I do terrible things to them. You can start by telling them who you really are."

"Why not?" said the man. "It's not as if they will be around to tell anyone else."

"You tell it, Mr. Cavendish," said the woman. "You have always had a way with words."

"But you have always been the better story-teller, Mrs. Cavendish, and I won't have you putting yourself down."

"And I thank you kindly for saying that, my dear, but . . ."

"Get on with it!" said the Jonah.

"We are older than we look," said the man. "We have assumed many names and identities, down the years, but we are perhaps still best known for our original nom de guerre, in the nineteenth century—the Murder Masques."

"Yes," said the woman, smiling for the first time as she took in our expressions. "That was us. Uncontested crime lords of old London, the greatest villains of the Victorian Age. No sin was ever practiced there, but we took our commission. We laughed at police and politicans. We even brought down the great Julien Advent himself."

"Or rather, you did," said the man. "Credit where credit is due, my very dear."

"But I couldn't have done it without you, dearest. Now, where was I? Ah yes. We became involved with corruption in business, along with everyone else, and discovered to our surprise that there was far more money to be made in business than in crime, if business was approached with the right attitude. So we put aside our famous masques, cut off our old contacts, and made new names for ourselves in Trade. We prospered, mostly at the expense of our more timid competitors, and soon enough we became a Corporation. And as corporations are immortal, so we became immortal. Such things happen, in the Nightside. As our business thrives, so do we. As long as it exists, so shall we. Money is power, power is magic. And, of course, when the well-being of Cavendish Properties is threatened, so are we."

"So we take all such threats very seriously," said the man. "And we take all necessary steps to defend ourselves."

"You're just vultures," said Dead Boy. "Profiting from the weaknesses of others, feeding on the carcasses of those you bring down."

"The very best kind of business," said Mrs. Cavendish. "Born of the Age of Capitalism, we now embody it."

"That's why you call yourself Mr. and Mrs. all the time," I said, just to feel I was contributing something. "Because you've had so many identities, you have to keep reminding yourselves who you are these days."

"True," said Mr. Cavendish. "But irrelevant."

"Julien Advent will track you down," I said. "He's never forgotten you."

The Cavendishes shared a warm smile. "And we have never forgotten him," said the woman. "Because there's one part of the story, that oft-told legend, which dear Julien has never got around to telling. The great love of his life, the one who betrayed him to the Murder Masques and their waiting Timeslip, was me. I shall never forget the look of shock and horror on his face when I took off my Masque. I thought I'd never be able to stop laughing."

"He cried," said the man. "Indeed he did. Real tears. But then Julien always was a sentimental sort."

"He really had no-one but himself to blame," said the woman. "I was working as a dancer in the chorus line when he met me. Just another pretty face with an average voice and a good pair of legs, but he took a fancy to me. Gentlemen often did, in those days. He introduced me to a better life, to all sorts of expensive tastes and appetites. Some of which he proved unwilling to provide. He thought he was saving me. He should have asked me whether I wanted to be saved.

"Since he wouldn't give me what I wanted, I went looking for someone who would, and at one of Julien's soirees, I made the acquaintance of the generous gentleman at my side. The Murder Masque himself. He showed me a whole new world of monies and pleasures, and I took to it as to the manner born. And so I took up a Masque, too, and I found far more thrills as a lord of crime than I ever did in poor Julien's arms. In the end, when I pushed him into the Timeslip to be rid of him, I didn't feel anything at all."

"Tell them," the Jonah said impatiently. "Tell John what we did to Rossignol. I want to see his face, once he realises there's nothing he can do to save her."

"Our Rossignol grew just a little too independent as she became more popular," said Mr. Cavendish. He sounded stiff and even bored, as though he was only saying this to satisfy the Jonah's wishes. "She started taking meetings on her own, without consulting us first. Executives at the record companies professed to be concerned by the terms of our deal, though Rossignol had been glad enough to sign it at the time, when no-one else would touch her. Those executives assured Rossignol she could do much better with them. They promised their lawyers would easily break the contract, if she would only transfer her allegiance to them. So she came to us and demanded a better deal, or she would leave."

"The impudence of the girl!" said Mrs. Cavendish. "Of course, we couldn't allow her to do any such thing. Not after all the money we'd already invested in her. And all the money we stood to make. We found her, we made her, we groomed her. We made Rossignol into a viable product. We had a right to protect our investment. Don't think you're fighting the good fight here, Mr. Taylor. This damsel in distress doesn't need rescuing. From what, after all? Fame and fortune? We promised we would make her a star, and so we shall. But she is our property, and no-one else's."

"What about freedom of choice?" I said.

"What about it?" said Mr. Cavendish. "This is business we're talking about. Rossignol signed away all such nonsense when she put her fate in our hands. Rossignol belongs to Cavendish Properties."

"Is that why you murdered her?" said Dead Boy. "Because she wanted to leave and run her own life?"

The Cavendishes didn't seem at all surprised by the accusation. If anything, they preened a little.

"We didn't actually kill her," said the woman.

"Not quite," said the man.

"She isn't entirely dead," said the woman. "The poison we gave her took her to the very edge of death, then the Jonah found and imposed the one chance in a million that held her there, at death's very door, in an extended Near-Death Experience. And when she came back from the edge, and we revived her, the profound shock had reduced her will and vitality to such a malleable state that she imprinted on us and accepted us as surrogate parents and authority figures. We had to keep her isolated, of course, to preserve this useful emotional connection. But even so, she persisted in displaying annoying signs of independence . . . perhaps we need to poison her again and repeat the process, to put her back in the right frame of mind."

"You bastards," said Rossignol.

"Oh hush, child," said the man. "Artistes never know what's best for them."

"But the best bit," said the Jonah, beaming happily, "the best bit is that only my will holds her where she is, on the very edge of death. My magic, my power. Her life is irrevocably linked to mine now. If you attack me, John, if you kill me, she goes all the way into the dark. Forever and ever. You don't dare threaten me."

"That's as may be," Dead Boy said mildly. "But what can you threaten me with? I only just met this girl, and her life and death are a small thing to me. You, on the other hand, have dared to meddle in my province, and I won't have that. I think I'll kill you anyway, Billy boy."

"Don't call me that! That's not my name any more! I'm . . ."

"The same irritating little tit you've always been, Billy."

"I'll . . ."

"You'll what? Kill me dead? Been there, done that, stole the T-shirt. And you're nowhere near powerful enough to break the compact I made."

"Perhaps not," said the Jonah, and suddenly he was smiling again. I stirred uneasily. I really didn't like that smile. The Jonah stepped forward to lock glares with Dead Boy. "You've done a really good job of stitching and stapling yourself together, down the years. All the wounds and damage you took, and never thought twice. Holding your battered and broken body together with superglue and duct tape. But . . . what if none of it had ever held? What if all your repairs just . . . failed?"

He made a short chopping gesture with one hand, and it was as though Dead Boy's body exploded. His back arched as black duct tape suddenly unwrapped and sailed away like streamers. Stitches and staples shot out, pattering softly to the stage, and his clothes were only tatters. No blood flew, or any other liquid, but all at once there were gaping wounds opening everywhere in Dead Boy's death-white flesh. He collapsed as his legs failed him, pale pink organs and guts falling out of him, and he hit the stage hard. One hand fell away entirely, the fingers still twitching. Dead Boy lay still, wounds opening slowly like flowers. I'd never realised how much damage he'd taken. Rossignol gripped my arm so hard it hurt, but didn't make a sound. And I just stood where I was, because I couldn't think of a single damned thing I could do to help my friend.

"Entropy," the Jonah said smugly, "means *everything* falls apart. Look at you now, Dead Boy. Not so big now, are you? Can you still feel pain? I do hope so. You must have made a hell of a deal, to be able to survive so much punishment . . . Not that it's done you any good, in the end. Tell you what, Mr. and Mrs. Cavendish, why don't you come over here and do the honours. Send him on his way. I wouldn't want to be accused of hogging all the fun."

The Cavendishes looked at each other, sighed quietly, then moved forward to indulge the Jonah. They stood over Dead Boy and studied his stubbornly existing body with thoughtful frowns.

"We could always feed him into a furnace," said Mr. Cavendish.

"Indeed we could," said Mrs. Cavendish. "I always enjoy it so much more when they're still alive to appreciate what's happening."

"But I think a more immediate end is called for here," said the man. "Major players like Dead Boy have a habit of escaping their fates, if given the slightest chance."

"And we haven't existed this long by taking unnecessary chances with our enemies, Mr. Cavendish."

"Quite right, my dear."

They both drew handguns from hidden holsters and shot Dead Boy in the heart and in the forehead. He jerked convulsively, pink-and-grey brains spraying out the back of his head. And then he lay back and was perfectly still, and his eyes looked at nothing at all. The Cavendishes turned to face me, and I gave them my best sneer.

"Your guns don't have bullets in them any more, you bastards."

The Cavendishes pulled the triggers anyway a few times, but nothing happened. They shrugged pretty much in unison and went back to stand behind their Jonah.

"We've always believed in delegation," said the man.

"You wanted him, dear Billy," said the woman. "He's all yours."

The Jonah stepped forward, smiling his cocky smile like he had all the time in the world and wouldn't have rushed this for anything. "Still got a few tricks left up your sleeve, eh, John? But then, tricks are all you ever really had. Your precious gift for finding things was never a real power, not like mine. There's nothing you can do to stop me killing you and taking Rossignol back where she belongs. How shall I kill you, John? Let me count the ways . . . The cancers that lie in wait, needing only a nudge to swell and prosper. The arthritis that lurks in every joint, the bacteria and viruses to boil in your blood . . . Perhaps all of them at once might be amusing. You might even explode like Dead

Boy! Or maybe . . . I'll find that one-in-a-million chance where you were born horribly deformed and helpless, and leave you like that. So everyone can see what happens to anyone foolish enough to cross the Jonah."

He could do it. He had the power. And all I had was a gift I didn't dare use again. Now my enemies knew exactly where I was, if I opened my mind to use my gift, they'd attack my mind directly. They'd take control of my mind and my soul in a second, then . . . there are worse things than death, in the Nightside. But without my gift, I didn't have anything strong enough to stop the Jonah and save Rossignol. All I had . . . was myself. I smiled suddenly, and the Jonah's grin faltered.

"Billy, Billy," I said, calm and easy and utterly condescending, "you never did understand the true nature of magic. It's not based in the power we wield or the gifts we inherit. In the end, it all comes down to will and intent. And the mind and soul behind them."

I locked eyes with the Jonah, and he stood very still. The whole world narrowed down to just the two of us, eye to eye, will to will. All we were, brought out onto the brightly lit mental stage, peeling back the layers to show who and what we were at the core. And for all his power, and despite everything he'd done, Billy Lathem looked away first. He actually staggered back a few steps, breathing hard, his face pale and sweaty.

"Who the hell are you?" he whispered. "What are you? You're not human . . ."

"More human than you, you little prick," said Rossignol. She stepped past me, and when the Jonah looked at her, she sang right into his face. Her voice

was strong and true and potent, and she aimed it like
a weapon right at him. I fell quickly backwards, clap-
ping my hands to my ears. Beyond the Jonah, the
Cavendishes were retreating, too, and protecting their
ears. Rossignol sang, face to face with the Jonah—a
sad, sad song of love lost and lovers gone, and all the
secret betrayals of the heart. She sang directly at him,
and he couldn't look away, couldn't back away, like a
mouse hypnotized by a snake, like a fish on a hook. She
held him where he was, with a merciless song of violation and isolation and the corruption of talent. Everything that had been done to her, she threw back at him.
And the more she sang, the more it was the story of his
life, too. Of poor little Billy Lathem, who might have
been a Power and a Domination like his father, but had
never been anything more than a hired thug.

The Cavendishes huddled together for comfort, as
far away as they could get. I had my hands pressed so
tightly to my ears I thought my skull would collapse
under the pressure, and still the edges of the song
ripped and tore at me, till my heart felt it would tear
loose in my chest. Tears were running down my face.
And Billy Lathem, forced to face the truth at last,
whispered, *Daddy, I only wanted you to be proud of
me* . . . and disappeared. Air rushed in to fill the space
his body had occupied, as Billy turned his power on
himself and selected the one chance where he was
never born.

Rossignol stopped singing, though the power of her
voice still seemed to reverberate on the air. She swayed
suddenly on her feet, then collapsed. I grabbed her before she hit the floor, but caught off-balance, her
weight carried both of us down. I sat on the stage, hold-

ing her in my arms, and only then realised she was dying. Her breathing was slowing, and I could feel her heart counting down to zero. Only the Jonah's will had kept her from death's door, and with him gone her long-delayed destiny was finally catching up with her. Vitality drained out of her, as though someone had opened a tap. I held her to me fiercely, as though I could stop it going through sheer force of will, but that trick never works twice.

"I promised I'd save you," I said numbly.

"You promised me the truth," said Rossignol, with pale lips that hardly moved. "I'll have to settle for that. Not even the great and mighty John Taylor can keep all his promises."

And just like that, she was gone. She stopped talking, she stopped breathing, and all the life went out of her. I still held her in my arms, rocking her quietly, still trying to comfort her.

"Oh dear," said Mr. Cavendish. "What a pity. Now we'll have to start all over again, with someone else."

"Never mind, Mr. Cavendish," said the woman. "Third time lucky."

I looked up at them, and there was murder in my eyes. They started pushing bullets into their guns, but their hands were trembling. And then we all looked round, startled, as Dead Boy spoke. It was just a whisper, with most of his lungs gone, but it was still and quite clear in the quiet.

"It's not over yet," he said, staring blindly up at the ceiling. "Rossignol is dead, but not actually departed. Not yet. There's still time, John. Still time to save her, if you've got the will and the courage."

"How is it you're still with us?" I said, too numb to

be properly surprised. "Half of your insides are scattered across the stage. They blew your brains out, for God's sake!"

He chuckled briefly. An eerie, ghostly sound. "My body's been dead for years. It doesn't really need its internal organs any more. They don't serve any purpose. This body is just a shape I inhabit. A habit of living. Like eating and drinking and all the other things I do to help me pretend I'm still alive. You can still rescue Rossignol, John. I can use your life force to power a magic, to send both of us after her. Into the dark lands, the borderlands we pass through between this life and the next. When I died and came back, the door was left open a crack for me. I can go after her, but only a living soul can bring her back again. I won't lie to you, John. You could die, doing this. We could all go through that final door and never return. But if you're willing to try, if you're willing to give up all your remaining years in one last gamble, I promise you, we have a chance."

"You can really do this?" I said.

"I told you," said Dead Boy. "I know all there is to know about death."

"Ah, hell," I said. "I never let a client down yet."

"An attitude like that will get you killed," said Dead Boy.

"What if the Cavendishes attack us while we're gone? Destroy our bodies, so there's nothing left to come back to?"

"We'll be back the same moment we left. Or we won't be back at all."

"Do it," I said.

Dead Boy did it, and we both died.

• • •

Powered by all the remaining years of my life, Dead Boy and I went into the dark together, and for the first time I discovered there is a darkness even darker than the Nightside. A night that never ends, that never knew stars or a moon. The coldest cell, the longest fall. It was the absence of everything, except for me and Dead Boy. I was just a presence, without form or shape, a scream without a mouth to limit it, but I calmed somewhat as I sensed Dead Boy's presence. We spoke without voices, heard though there was no sound.

There's nothing here. Nothing . . .

Actually there is, John, but you're still too close to life to be able to appreciate it. Think yourself lucky.

Where's Ross?

Think of the darkness as a tunnel, leading us to a light. A way out. This way . . .

Yes . . . How can there be a direction when there's nothing . . .

Stop asking questions, John. You really wouldn't like the answers. Now follow me.

You've been this way before.

Part of me is always here.

Is that supposed to make me feel better? You're a real spooky person, you know that?

You have no idea, John. This way . . .

And we were falling in a whole new direction. It did help to think of the darkness as a tunnel, leading somewhere. We were definitely approaching something, though with no landmarks it was impossible to judge our speed or progress. I should have been scared, terrified, but already my emotions were fading away, as though they didn't belong there. Even my thoughts were growing fuzzy round the edges. But then I began to feel there was something ahead of me, something special, calling me. A speck of light appeared, beautiful and brilliant, all the colours of the rainbow in a single sharp moment of light. It grew unhurriedly, a great and glorious incandescence, yet still warm and comforting, like the golden beam from a lighthouse, bringing ships safely home through the long lonely nights. And then there was another presence with us, and it was Rossignol.

Are you angels?

Hardly, Ross. I don't think they're talking to me any more. This is John, with Dead Boy. We've come to take you home.

But I can hear music. Wonderful music. All the songs I ever wanted to sing.

For her it was music, for me it was light. Like the warm glow from a window, the friendly light of home after a long hard journey. Or pehaps the last light of the day, when all work is over, all responsibilities put aside, and we can all rest at last. Day is done. Welcome home, at last.

Oh John, I don't think I want to go back.

I know, Ross. I feel it, too. It's like . . . we've been playing a game, and now the game's over, and it's time to go back where we belong . . .

There was a sense of taking her hand in mine, and we moved towards the light and the music. But Dead Boy had been there before. Kindly, remorselessly, he took us both by the hand and pulled us away, back to life and bodies and all the worries of the world.

• • •

I sat up sharply, dragging air deep into my lungs as though I'd been underwater for ages. The lesser light of the world crashed in around me. I'd never felt so clearly, starkly *alive*. My skin tingled with a hundred sensations, the world was full of sound, and Ross was right there beside me. She threw herself into my arms, and for a long moment we hugged each other like we'd never let go. But eventually we did and got to our feet again. We were back in the real world, with all its own demands and priorities. Dead Boy was standing before us, complete and intact again, resplendent in his undamaged finery. The only difference was the neat bullet hole in his forehead.

"Told you I know all there is to know about death," he said smugly. "Oh, I used some of your life energy to repair the damage the Jonah did to my body, John. Knew you wouldn't mind. Trust me, you won't miss it."

I glared at him. "Next time, ask."

Dead Boy raised an eyebrow. "I hope very much there isn't going to be a next time."

"Just how much of my life force did we use up on this stunt anyway?"

"Surprisingly little. It seems there is more to you than meets the eye, John. Mind you, there would have to be."

"You were dead!" said Mr. Cavendish, just a little shrilly. He sounded like he might be going to cry. "You were all dead, and now you're alive again! It just isn't fair!"

"That's the trouble with the Nightside," Mrs. Cavendish said sulkily. "You can't rely on people staying dead. Next time, do remember to bring some thermite bombs with us."

"Quite right, Mrs. Cavendish. Still, they all look decidedly weakened by whatever unnaural thing it was they just did, so I think it's back to the old reliable bullet in the head. Lots of them, this time."

"Exactly, Mr. Cavendish. If we can't have Rossignol, no-one can."

They aimed their reloaded guns at her. I moved to put myself between her and the guns, but that was all I could do. My time in the dark had taken everything else out of me, for the moment. I looked at Dead Boy, who shrugged.

"Sorry, I'm running on empty, too. Rossignol, any chance of a song?"

"Darling, right now I couldn't even squeak out a note. There must be something we can do!"

"Oh, shut up and die," said Mrs. Cavendish.

The two of them approached us, guns extended, taking their time, enjoying seeing their enemies helpless before them. They were going to shoot us all, and I had no magics left to stop them. But I've never relied on magic to get me through the many and varied dangers of the Nightside. I've always found using my wits and being downright sneaky much more reliable. So I waited till the Cavendishes were right in front of me, then I dug a good handful of pepper out of my hidden stash and threw it right into their smug, smiling faces. They both screamed pitifully as the pepper ground into their eyes, and I slapped the guns out of their flailing hands and gave the two of them a good smack round the back of the head, just on general principles. Dead Boy kicked their feet out from under them, and they ended up sitting on the stage, huddled together and clawing frantically at their streaming eyes.

"Condiments," I said easily. "Never leave home without them. And once the Authorities get here, I'll rub salt into your wounds as well."

At which point, an unconscious combat magician came flying onto the stage from the wings, upside down and bleeding heavily. He'd barely hit the stage with a resounding thud before two more combat magicians were backing quickly onto the stage, retreating from an unseen foe. Zen magics spat and shimmered on the air before them, as their rapidly moving hands wove cat's cradles of defensive magics. But Julien Advent, the great Victorian Adventurer himself, was more than a match for them. He bounded onstage with marvelous energy, dodging the thrown spells with practiced skill, and proceeded to run rings around the bewildered combat magicians with breathtaking acrobatics and vicious fisticuffs. He moved almost too quickly to be seen, impossibly graceful, smiling all the time, smiting down the ungodly with magnificent ease.

Being an editor for thirty years didn't seem to have slowed him down at all.

He finally stood over three unconscious combat magicians, not even breathing hard, the bastard. Dead Boy and Ross and I applauded him because, you had to, really. Julien Advent actually was all the things they said he was. He shot me a quick grin as he took in the defeated Cavendishes.

"I see the cavalry probably wasn't needed after all. Good work, John. We were afraid we might be a little overdue."

I'd only just started to process the word *we* and get

the beginnings of a really bad feeling, when Walker strolled on from the wings, and all I could think was *Oh shit. I'm really in trouble now.*

Walker strode over to consider the weeping, red-eyed Cavendishes, his face as always completely calm and utterly unreadable. Walker, in his neat city suit and bowler hat, representative of the Authorities, and quite possibly the most dangerous man in the Nightside. He had been given power over everyone and everything in the Nightside, and if you were wise, you didn't ask by whom. I would have run like hell, if I'd had any strength left.

The Cavendishes became aware of Julien's presence. They forced themselves up onto their feet and faced him defiantly. He studied their faces for a long moment, his smile gone, his eyes cold.

"I've always known who you were," he said finally. "The infamous Murder Masques, still villains, still unpunished. But I could never prove it, until now." He looked at me. "I knew if anyone could bring them down, it would be you, John. If only because you were too dumb to know it was impossible. So after you came to me, I contacted Walker, and we've been following you ever since. At a discreet distance, of course. We even stood in the wings and listened as the Cavendishes incriminated themselves with their gloating. It was all so very interesting I almost didn't hear the combat magicians until it was too late. I should have known the Cavendishes would bring backup."

"I speak for the Authorities," Walker said to the Cavendishes. "And I say you're history."

"It all began with them," said Julien. "They Time-slipped me because they wanted to sieze my transformational potion, as their first big business venture. Typical, really. They couldn't just earn their money. They had to cheat. Little good it did them, because it was only after I was gone, slammed eighty years into the future in a moment, that they discovered there was no formula anywhere among my notes. I'd kept all the details in my head."

He stopped then and looked directly at Mrs. Cavendish. She stood a little straighter, still knuckling tears from one eye. The legendary Victorian Adventurer and his legendary lost love, the betrayed and the betrayer, face to face for the first time in over a century.

"Irene . . ."

"Julien."

"You haven't changed at all."

"Oh, don't look at me. I look awful."

"I've always known it was you. Hidden behind your new names and identities."

"Then why did you never come for me?"

"Because even the greatest love will die, if you stick a sharp enough knife through its heart. I knew it was you, but I couldn't prove it. You and your husband were very well protected. And in the end, I just didn't care any more. It was all such a long time ago, and I never did believe in living in the past."

She gaped at him, almost horrified. "All those years we spent waiting for you to come after us. Spinning webs and layers of protections around us, always hiding . . . all those years of being afraid of you, and you didn't give a damn."

"I had a new life to build, Irene. And there were far

worse things than you in the Nightside that needed fighting."

She looked away. "I thought, sometimes, that you might have held back . . . because of me."

"My love died a long time ago. I don't know you now, Irene."

"You never did, Julien."

Mr. Cavendish moved in possessively beside his wife. "Enough talk! We all know why you're here! Have your precious revenge and be done with it! Kill us, for everything we did to you!"

"You never did understand me," said Julien. He looked at Walker. "Take them away. Destroy their business, dismantle it, and you destroy their power. Bring them to trial and send them down. Make them into little people, like all the ones they hurt. What better punishment, for such as these?"

"I'd be delighted," said Walker, tipping his bowler hat to Julien. "My people are already on their way."

Julien gave Walker a hard, thoughtful look. "These two probably know all sorts of top people and secrets. Don't let them wriggle out."

"Not going to happen," Walker said easily. "I've been looking for an excuse to bring the Cavendishes down. Trouble-makers, always rocking the boat, never playing well with others. They might even have become a threat to the Authorities, in time. And we can't have that, can we?"

He turned unhurriedly to look at me, and I braced myself. "Well, John," said Walker. "You've led me quite a chase. Who's been a bad boy, then? But . . . not to worry. Helping me put away two big fish like these goes a long way to making up for all the trouble you've caused the Nightside tonight. Only just, mind . . ."

Julien looked at me sharply, suddenly scenting a story. "John, what is he talking about?"

"Haven't a clue," I lied, cheerfully.

TEN

Coda, with a Dying Fall

A week later, I caught Rossignol's new set at Caliban's Cavern. It was a sell-out, she was singing up a storm, and the audience loved it.

A lot had changed in the past week. The Cavendishes had had to sell Caliban's Cavern, for quick cash, to help them pay their mounting legal bills. The charges against them were building all the time, with more and more people coming out of the wood-work to kick the Cavendishes while they were safely down. It was fast becoming the Nightside's favourite sport.

Rossignol was under new management. Some group of show business lawyers who knew a good thing when they heard it and were wise enough to present Rossignol with a reasonably fair contract. They were putting a lot of money behind her, and the word was she was going to break big. She was already recording her first album, with a respected big-name producer.

The club that night was really swinging. The audience packed the place from wall to wall and danced in the aisles. It was a more usual mix this time, with hardly any of the old Goth element. Rossignol was moving upmarket with her new material. I was there on my own. Dead Boy was off working on another case, and Julien Advent had a paper to put out. I could have asked my secretary Cathy, but she'd lost interest in Rossignol once she'd gone mainstream. Cathy was strictly cutting-edge only.

Backed by two Ian Augers, a new drummer, and all new backing singers, Rossignol sang of love and light and rebirth in her clear glorious voice, touching the hearts of all who heard her. She was strong and vibrant and magnificently alive. She still hung off the microphone stand and smoked like a chimney, though. The crowd loved her. She took three encores, to rapturous applause, and nobody even looked like they were thinking of killing themselves. It's nice when a case has a happy ending.

After the show, I went round the back to her dressing room. To my surprise, the door was being guarded by Dead Boy. He had the grace to look just a little embarrassed.

"So, this is your new case," I said. "No wonder you didn't want to talk about it. Bodyguarding is a bit of a step down for you, isn't it?"

"It's only temporary," he said with great dignity.

"Until she and her new management can agree on someone they trust."

"She could have asked me," I said.

"Ah," said Dead Boy. "John, she's trying to forget what happened. You can't blame her, really."

"What happened to the bullet hole in your forehead?" I said, deliberately changing the subject.

"Filled it in with builder's putty," he said briskly. "Once I've grown my hair out a bit, you'll never notice it."

"And the hole in the back?"

"Don't ask."

I knocked on the dressing room door and went in. The room was full of flowers. I would have brought some, but I never think of these things. Rossignol was taking off her make-up in front of the mirror. She didn't seem particularly pleased to see me. She gave me a quick hug, kissed the air near my cheek, and we sat down facing each other. Her face was flushed, and she was still a little breathless from the set.

"Thank you for all your help, John. I do appreciate it, really. I would have phoned, but I've been very busy putting the new set together."

"I was out there," I said. "It went over great."

"It did, didn't it? John . . . don't take this wrong, but, I don't want to see you again."

"There doesn't seem any good way to take it," I said, after a moment. "What brought this on, Ross?"

"You remind me too much of bad times," she said bluntly. "I need to move on, leave it all behind. Now I'm alive again, I see things differently. I live only to sing. It's all I've ever wanted or needed. There's no room for anyone else in my life, right now. And especially not for you, John. I am grateful for everything you've done, but . . . as near as possible, I want to live a normal life now. I'm not staying in the Nightside. It was only ever somewhere to make a start. I'm going places, John."

"Yes," I said.

"I'll write a song about you, someday."

"That would be nice."

She turned away and started removing her make-up again, pulling faces at herself in the mirror. "You never did say—who hired you to look after me?"

"It was your father."

She looked at me sharply. "John, my father's been dead for two years now."

She dug into her bag and found an old photo. It was unmistakably the man who'd come into Strangefellows to hire me. So—a ghost. Not all that unusual, for the Nightside. Rossignol was touched.

"He always was very protective."

"Well," I said, "I guess I don't get paid for this case, either."

I gave Rossignol a good-bye kiss, wished her all the luck in the world, and left her dressing room. Humming the blues.

Sookie Stackhouse should have known that getting
intimately involved with a vampire wasn't a
good idea . . .

DEAD TO THE WORLD

Turn the page and take a bite out of Charlaine Harris's
acclaimed Sookie Stackhouse series, and find out why
this sexy mystery is going to knock 'em dead. Or undead,
as the case may be . . .

Now available from Ace Books!

The New Year's Eve party at Merlotte's Bar and Grill was finally, finally, over. Though the bar owner, Sam Merlotte, had asked all his staff to work that night, Holly, Arlene, and I were the only ones who'd responded. Charlsie Tooten had said she was too old to put up with the mess we had to endure on New Year's Eve, Danielle had long-standing plans to attend a fancy party with her steady boyfriend, and a new woman couldn't start for two days. I guess Arlene and Holly and I needed the money more than we needed a good time.

And I hadn't had any invitations to do anything else. At least when I'm working at Merlotte's, I'm a part of the scenery. That's a kind of acceptance.

I was sweeping up the shredded paper, and I reminded myself again not to comment to Sam on what a poor idea the bags of confetti had been. We'd all made ourselves pretty clear about that, and even good-natured Sam was showing signs of wear and tear. It didn't seem fair to leave it all for Terry Bellefleur to clean, though sweeping and mopping the floors was his job.

Sam was counting the till money and bagging it up so he could go by the night deposit at the bank. He was looking tired but pleased.

He flicked open his cell phone. "Kenya? You ready to take me to the bank? Okay, see you in a minute at the back door." Kenya, a police officer, often escorted Sam to the night deposit, especially after a big take like tonight's.

I was pleased with my money take, too. I had earned a lot in tips. I thought I might have gotten three hundred dollars or more—and I needed every penny. I would have enjoyed the prospect of totting up the money when I got home, if I'd been sure I had enough brains left to do it. The noise and chaos of the party, the constant runs to and from the bar and the serving hatch, the tremendous mess we'd had to clean up, the steady cacophony of all those brains . . . it had combined to exhaust me. Toward the end I'd been too tired to keep my poor mind protected, and lots of thoughts had leaked through.

It's not easy being telepathic. Most often, it's not fun.

This evening had been worse than most. Not only had the bar patrons, almost all known to me for many years, been in uninhibited moods, but there'd been some news that lots of people were just dying to tell me.

"I hear yore boyfriend done gone to South America," a car salesman, Chuck Beecham, had said, malice gleaming in his eyes. "You gonna get mighty lonely out to your place without him."

"You offering to take his place, Chuck?" the man beside him at the bar had asked, and they both had a we're-men-together guffaw.

"Naw, Terrell," said the salesman. "I don't care for vampire leavings."

"You be polite, or you go out the door," I said steadily. I felt warmth at my back, and I knew my boss, Sam Merlotte, was looking at them over my shoulder.

"Trouble?" he asked.

"They were just about to apologize," I said, looking Chuck and Terrell in the eyes. They looked down at their beers.

"Sorry, Sookie," Chuck mumbled, and Terrell bobbed his head in agreement. I nodded and turned to take care of another order. But they'd succeeded in hurting me.

Which was their goal.

I had an ache around my heart.

I was sure the general populace of Bon Temps, Louisiana, didn't know about our estrangement. Bill sure wasn't in the habit of blabbing his personal business around, and neither was I. Arlene and Tara knew a little about it, of course, since you have to tell your best friends when you've broken up with your guy, even if you have to leave out all the interesting details. (Like the fact that you'd killed the woman he left you for. Which I couldn't help. Really.) So anyone who told me Bill had gone out of the country, assuming I didn't know it yet, was just being malicious.

Until Bill's recent visit to my house, I'd last seen him when I'd given him the disks and computer he'd hidden with me. I'd driven up at dusk, so the machine wouldn't be sitting on his front porch for long. I'd put all his stuff up against the door in a big waterproofed box. He'd come out just as I was driving away, but I hadn't stopped.

An evil woman would have given the disks to Bill's boss, Eric. A lesser woman would have kept those disks and that computer, having rescinded Bill's (and Eric's) invitations to enter the house. I had told myself proudly that I was not an evil, or a lesser, woman.

Also, thinking practically, Bill could just have hired some human to break into my house and take them. I didn't think he would. But he needed them bad, or he'd be in trouble with his boss's boss. I've got a temper, maybe even a bad temper, once it gets provoked. But I'm not vindictive.

Arlene has often told me I am too nice for my own good, though I assure her I am not. (Tara never says that; maybe she knows me better?) I realized glumly that, sometime during this hectic evening, Arlene would hear about Bill's departure. Sure enough, within twenty minutes of Chuck and Terrell's gibing, she made her way through the crowd to pat me on the back. "You didn't need that cold bastard anyway," she said. "What did he ever do for you?"

I nodded weakly at her to show how much I appreciated her support. But then a table called for two whiskey sours, two beers, and a gin and tonic, and I had to hustle, which was actually a welcome distraction. When I dropped off their drinks, I asked myself the same question. What had Bill done for me?

I delivered pitchers of beer to two tables before I could add it all up.

He'd introduced me to sex, which I really enjoyed. Introduced me to a lot of other vampires, which I didn't. Saved my life, though when you thought about it, it wouldn't have been in danger if I hadn't been dating him in the first place. But I'd saved his back once or twice, so that debt was canceled. He'd called me "sweetheart," and at the time he'd meant it.

"Nothing," I muttered, as I mopped up a spilled piña colada and handed one of our last clean bar towels to the woman who'd knocked it over, since a lot of it was still in her skirt. "He didn't do a thing for me." She smiled and nodded, obviously thinking I was commiserating with her. The place was too noisy to hear anything, anyway, which was lucky for me.

But I'd be glad when Bill got back. After all, he was my nearest neighbor. The community's older cemetery separated our properties, which lay along a parish road south of Bon Temps. I was out there all by myself, without Bill.

"Peru, I hear," my brother, Jason, said. He had his arm around his girl of the evening, a short, thin, dark twenty-one-year-old from somewhere way out in the sticks. (I'd carded her.) I gave her a close look. Jason didn't know it, but she was a shape-shifter of some kind. They're easy to spot. She was an attractive girl, but she changed into something with feathers or fur when the moon was full. I noticed Sam give her a hard glare when Jason's back was turned, to remind her to behave herself in his territory. She returned the glare, with interest. I had the feeling she didn't become a kitten, or a squirrel.

I thought of latching on to her brain and trying to read it, but shifter heads aren't easy. Shifter thoughts are kind of snarly and red, though every now and then you can get a good picture of emotions. Same with Weres.

Sam himself turns into a collie when the moon is bright and round. Sometimes he trots all the way over to my house, and I feed him a bowl of scraps and let him nap on my back porch, if the weather's good, or in my living room, if the weather's poor. I don't let him in the bedroom anymore, because he wakes up naked—in which state he looks *very* nice, but I just don't need to be tempted by my boss.

The moon wasn't full tonight, so Jason would be safe. I decided not to say anything to him about his date. Everyone's got a secret or two. Her secret was just a little more colorful.

Besides my brother's date, and Sam of course, there were two other supernatural creatures in Merlotte's Bar that New Year's Eve. One was a magnificent woman at least six feet tall, with long rippling dark hair. Dressed to kill in a skintight long-sleeved orange dress, she'd come in by herself, and she was in the process of meeting every guy in the bar. I didn't know what she was, but I knew from her brain pattern that she was not human. The other creature was a vampire, who'd come in with a group of young people, most in their early twenties. I didn't know any of them. Only a sideways glance by a few other revelers marked the presence of a vampire. It just went to show the change in attitude in the few years since the Great Revelation.

Almost three years ago, on the night of the Great Revelation, the vampires had gone on TV in every nation to announce their existence. It had been a night in which many of the world's assumptions had been knocked sideways and rearranged for good.

This coming-out party had been prompted by the Japanese development of a synthetic blood that can keep vamps satisfied nutritionally. Since the Great Revelation, the United States has undergone numerous political and social upheavals in the bumpy process of accommodating our newest citizens, who just happen to be dead. The vampires have a public face and a public explanation for their condition— they claim an allergy to sunlight, and garlic causes severe metabolic changes—but I've seen the other side of the vampire world. My eyes now see a lot of things most human beings don't ever see. Ask me if this knowledge has made me happy.

No.

But I have to admit, the world is a more interesting place to me now. I'm by myself a lot (since I'm not exactly Norma Normal), so the extra food for thought has been welcome. The fear and danger haven't. I've seen the private face of vampires, and I've learned about Weres and shifters and other stuff. Weres and shifters prefer to stay in the shadows—for now— while they watch how going public works out for the vamps.

See, I had all this to mull over while collecting tray after tray of glasses and mugs, and unloading and loading the dishwasher to help Tack, the new cook. (His real name is Alphonse Petacki. Can you be surprised he likes "Tack" better?) When our part of the cleanup was just about finished, and this long evening was finally over, I hugged Arlene and wished her a happy New Year, and she hugged me back. Holly's boyfriend was waiting for her at the employees' entrance at the back of the building, and Holly waved to us as she pulled on her coat and hurried out.

"What're your hopes for the New Year, ladies?" Sam asked. By that time, Kenya was leaning against the bar, waiting for him, her face calm and alert. Kenya ate lunch here pretty regularly with her partner, Kevin, who was as pale and thin as she was dark and rounded. Sam was putting the chairs up on the tables so Terry Bellefleur, who came in very early in the morning, could mop the floor.

"Good health, and the right man," Arlene said dramatically, her hands fluttering over her heart, and we laughed. Arlene has found many men—and she's been married four times—but she's still looking for Mr. Right. I could "hear" Arlene thinking that Tack might be the one. I was startled; I hadn't even known she'd looked at him.

The surprise showed on my face, and in an uncertain voice Arlene said, "You think I should give up?"

"Hell, no," I said promptly, chiding myself for not guarding my expression better. It was just that I was so tired. "It'll be this year, for sure, Arlene." I smiled at Bon Temp's only black female police officer. "You have to have a wish for the New Year, Kenya. Or a resolution."

"I always wish for peace between men and

women," Kenya said. "Make my job a lot easier. And my resolution is to bench-press one-forty."

"Wow," said Arlene. Her dyed red hair contrasted violently with Sam's natural curly red-gold as she gave him a quick hug. He wasn't much taller than Arlene—though she's at least five foot eight, two inches taller than I. "I'm going to lose ten pounds, that's my resolution." We all laughed. That had been Arlene's resolution for the past four years. "What about you, Sam? Wishes and resolutions?" she asked.

"I have everything I need," he said, and I felt the blue wave of sincerity coming from him. "I resolve to stay on this course. The bar is doing great, I like living in my double-wide, and the people here are as good as people anywhere."

I turned to conceal my smile. That had been a pretty ambiguous statement. The people of Bon Temps were, indeed, as good as people anywhere.

"And you, Sookie?" he asked. Arlene, Kenya, and Sam were all looking at me. I hugged Arlene again, because I like to. I'm ten years younger—maybe more, since though Arlene says she's thirty-six, I have my doubts—but we've been friends ever since we started working at Merlotte's together after Sam bought the bar, maybe five years now.

"Come on," Arlene said, coaxing me. Sam put his arm around me. Kenya smiled, but drifted away into the kitchen to have a few words with Tack.

Acting on impulse, I shared my wish. "I just hope to not be beaten up," I said, my weariness and the hour combining in an ill-timed burst of honesty. "I don't want to go to the hospital. I don't want to see a doctor." I didn't want to have to ingest any vampire blood, either, which would cure you in a hurry but had various side effects. "So my resolution is to stay out of trouble," I said firmly.

Arlene looked pretty startled, and Sam looked—well, I couldn't tell about Sam. But since I'd hugged Arlene, I gave him a big hug, too, and felt the strength and warmth in his body. You think Sam's slight until you see him shirtless unloading boxes of supplies. He is really strong and built really smooth, and he has a high natural body temperature. I felt him kiss my hair, and then we were all saying good night to each other and walking out the back door. Sam's truck was parked in front of his trailer, which is set up behind Merlotte's Bar but at a right angle to it, but he climbed in Kenya's patrol car to ride to the bank. She'd bring him home, and then Sam would collapse. He'd been on his feet for hours, as had we all.

As Arlene and I unlocked our cars, I noticed Tack was waiting in his old pickup; I was willing to bet he was going to follow Arlene home.

With a last "Good night!" called through the chilly silence of the Louisiana night, we separated to begin our new years.

I turned off onto Hummingbird Road to go out to my place, which is about three miles southeast of the bar. The relief of finally being alone was immense, and I began to relax mentally. My headlights flashed past the close-packed trunks of the pines that formed the backbone of the lumber industry hereabouts.

The night was extremely dark and cold. There are no streetlights way out on the parish roads, of course. Creatures were not stirring, not by any means. Though I kept telling myself to be alert for deer crossing the road, I was driving on autopilot. My simple thoughts were filled with the plan of scrubbing my face and pulling on my warmest nightgown and climbing into my bed.

Something white appeared in the headlights of my old car.

I gasped, jolted out of my drowsy anticipation of warmth and silence.

A running man: At three in the morning on January first, he was running down the parish road, apparently running for his life.

I slowed down, trying to figure out a course of action. I was a lone unarmed woman. If something awful was pursuing him, it might get me, too. On the other hand, I couldn't let someone suffer if I could help. I had a moment to notice that the man was tall, blond, and clad only in blue jeans, before I pulled up by him. I put the car into park and leaned over to roll down the window on the passenger's side.

"Can I help you?" I called. He gave me a panicked glance and kept on running.

But in that moment I realized who he was. I leaped out of the car and took off after him.

"Eric!" I yelled. "It's me!"

He wheeled around then, hissing, his fangs fully out. I stopped so abruptly I swayed where I stood, my hands out in front of me in a gesture of peace. Of course, if Eric decided to attack, I was a dead woman. So much for being a good Samaritan.

Why didn't Eric recognize me? I'd known him for many months. He was Bill's boss, in the complicated vampire hierarchy that I was beginning to learn. Eric was the sheriff of Area Five, and he was a vampire on the rise. He was also gorgeous and could kiss like a house afire, but that was not the most pertinent side of him right at the moment. Fangs and strong hands curved into claws were what I was seeing. Eric was in full alarm mode, but he seemed just as scared of me as I was of him. He didn't leap to attack.

"Stay back, woman," he warned me. His voice sounded like his throat was sore, raspy and raw.

"What are you doing out here?"

"Who are you?"

"You known darn good and well who I am. What's up with you? Why are you out here without your car?" Eric drove a sleek Corvette, which was simply Eric.

"You know me? Who am I?"

Well, that knocked me for a loop. He sure didn't sound like he was joking. I said cautiously, "Of course I know you, Eric. Unless you have an identical twin. You don't, right?"

"I don't know." His arms dropped, his fangs seemed to be retracting, and he straightened from his crouch, so I felt there'd been a definite improvement in the atmosphere of our encounter.

"You don't know if you have a brother?" I was pretty much at sea.

"No. I don't know. Eric is my name?" In the glare of my headlights, he looked just plain pitiful.

"Wow." I couldn't think of anything more helpful to say. "Eric Northman is the name you go by these days. Why are you out here?"

"I don't know that, either."

I was sensing a theme here. "For real? You don't remember anything?" I tried to get past being sure that at any second he'd grin down at me and explain everything and laugh, embroiling me in some trouble that would end in me . . . getting beaten up.

"For real." He took a step closer, and his bare white chest made me shiver with sympathetic goose bumps. I also realized (now that I wasn't terrified) how forlorn he looked. It was an expression I'd never seen on the confident Eric's face before, and it made me feel unaccountably sad.

"You know you're a vampire, right?"

"Yes." He seemed surprised that I asked. "And you are not."

"No. I'm real human, and I have to know you won't hurt me. Though you could have by now. But believe me, even if you don't remember it, we're sort of friends."

"I won't hurt you."

I reminded myself that probably hundreds and thousands of people had heard those very words before Eric ripped their throats out. But the fact is, vampires don't have to kill once they're past their first year. A sip here, a sip there, that's the norm. When he looked so lost, it was hard to remember he could dismember me with his bare hands.

I'd told Bill one time that the smart thing for aliens to do (when they invaded Earth) would be to arrive in the guise of lop-eared bunnies.

"Come get in my car before you freeze," I said. I was having that I'm-getting-sucked-in feeling again, but I didn't know what else to do.

"I do know you?" he said, as though he were hesitant about getting in a car with someone as formidable as a woman ten inches shorter, many pounds lighter, and a few centuries younger.

"Yes," I said, not able to restrain an edge of impatience. I wasn't too happy with myself, because I still half suspected I was being tricked for some unfathomable reason. "Now come on, Eric. I'm freezing, and so are you." Not that vampires seemed to feel temperature extremes, as a rule; but even Eric's skin looked goosey. The dead can freeze, of course. They'll survive it—they survive almost everything—but I understand it's pretty painful. "Oh my God, Eric, you're barefoot." I'd just noticed.

I took his hand; he let me get close enough for that. He let me lead him back to the car and stow him in the passenger seat. I told him to roll up the window as I went around to my side, and after a long minute of studying the mechanism, he did.

I reached in the backseat for an old afghan I keep there in the winter (for football games, etc.) and wrapped it around him. He wasn't shivering, of course, because he was a vampire, but I just couldn't stand to look at all that bare flesh in this temperature. I turned the heater on full blast (which, in my old car, isn't saying much).

Eric's exposed skin had never made me feel cold before—when I'd seen this much of Eric before, I'd felt anything *but*. I was giddy enough by now to laugh out loud before I could censor my own thoughts.

He was startled, and looked at me sideways.

"You're the last person I expected to see," I said. "Were you coming out this way to see Bill? Because he's gone."

"Bill?"

"The vampire who lives out here? My ex-boyfriend?"

He shook his head. He was back to being absolutely terrified.

"You don't know how you came to be here?"

He shook his head again.

I was making a big effort to think hard; but it was just that, an effort. I was worn out. Though I'd had a rush of adrenaline when I'd spotted the figure running down the dark road, that rush was wearing off fast. I reached the turnoff to my house and turned left, winding through the black and silent woods on my nice, level driveway—that, in fact, Eric had had re-graveled for me.

And that was why Eric was sitting in my car right now, instead of running through the night like a giant white rabbit. He'd had the intelligence to give me what I really wanted. (Of course, he'd also wanted me to go to bed with him for months. But he'd given me the driveway because I needed it.)

"Here we are," I said, pulling around to the back of my old house. I switched off the car. I'd remembered to leave the outside lights on when I'd left for work that afternoon, thank goodness, so we weren't sitting there in total darkness.

"This is where you live?" He was glancing around the clearing where the old house stood, seemingly nervous about going from the car to the back door.

"Yes," I said, exasperated.

He just gave me a look that showed white all around the blue of his eyes.

"Oh, come on," I said, with no grace at all. I got out of the car and went up the steps to the back porch, which I don't keep locked because, hey, why lock a screened-in back porch? I do lock the inner door, and after a second's fumbling, I had it open so the light I leave on in the kitchen could spill out. "You can come in," I said, so he could cross the threshold. He scuttled in after me, the afghan still clutched around him.

Under the overhead light in the kitchen, Eric looked pretty pitiful. His bare feet were bleeding, which I hadn't noticed before. "Oh, Eric," I said sadly, and got a pan out from the cabinet, and started the hot water to running in the sink. He'd heal real quick, like vampires do, but I couldn't help but wash him clean. The blue jeans were filthy around the hem. "Pull 'em off," I said, knowing they'd just get wet if I soaked his feet while he was dressed.

With not a hint of a leer or any other indication that he was enjoying this development, Eric shimmied out of the jeans. I tossed them onto the back porch to wash in the morning, trying not to gape at my guest, who was now clad in underwear that was definitely over-the-top, a bright red bikini style whose stretchy quality was definitely being tested. Okay, another big surprise. I'd seen Eric's underwear only once before—which was once more than I ought to have— and he'd been a silk boxers guy. Did men change styles like that?

Without preening, and without comment, the vampire rewrapped his white body in the afghan. Hmmm. I was now convinced he wasn't himself, as no other evidence could have convinced me. Eric was way over six feet of pure magnificence (if a marble white magnificence), and he well knew it.

I pointed to one of the straight-back chairs at the kitchen table. Obediently, he pulled it out and sat. I crouched to put the pan on the floor, and I gently guided his big feet into the water. Eric groaned as the warmth touched his skin. I guess that even a vampire could feel the contrast. I got a clean rag from under the sink and some liquid soap, and I washed his feet. I took my time, because I was trying to think what to do next.

"You were out in the night," he observed, in a tentative sort of way.

"I was coming home from work, as you can see from my clothes." I was wearing our winter uniform, a long-sleeved white boat-neck T-shirt with "Merlotte's Bar" embroidered over the left breast and worn tucked into black slacks.

"Women shouldn't be out alone this late at night," he said disapprovingly.

"Tell me about it."

"Well, women are more liable to be overwhelmed by an attack than men, so they should be more protected—"

"No, I didn't mean literally. I meant, I agree. You're preaching to the choir. I didn't want to be working this late at night."

"Then why were you out?"

"I need the money," I said, wiping my hand and pulling the roll of bills out of my pocket and dropping it on the table while I was thinking about it. "I got this house to maintain, my car is old, and I have taxes and insurance to pay. Like everyone else," I added, in case he thought I was complaining unduly. I hated to poormouth, but he'd asked.

"Is there no man in your family?"

Every now and then, their ages do show. "I have a brother. I can't remember if you've ever met Jason."

A cut on his left foot looked especially bad. I put some more hot water into the basin to warm the remainder. Then I tried to get all the dirt out. He winced as I gently rubbed the washcloth over the margins of the wound. The smaller cuts and bruises seemed to be fading even as I watched. The hot water heater came on behind me, the familiar sound somehow reassuring.

"Your brother permits you to do this working?"

I tried to imagine Jason's face when I told him that I expected him to support me for the rest of my life because I was a woman and shouldn't work outside the home. "Oh, for goodness sake, Eric." I looked up at him, scowling. "Jason's got his own problems." Like being chronically selfish and a true tomcat.

I eased the pan of water to the side and patted Eric dry with a dishtowel. This vampire now had clean feet. Rather stiffly, I stood. My back hurt. My feet hurt. "Listen, I think what I better do is call Pam. She'll probably know what's going on with you."

"Pam?"

It was like being around a particularly irritating two-year-old.

"Your second-in-command."

He was going to ask another question, I could just tell. I held up a hand. "Just hold on. Let me call her and find out what's happening."

"But what if she has turned against me?"

"Then we need to know that, too. The sooner the better."

I put my hand on the old phone that hung on the kitchen wall right by the end of the counter. A high stool sat below it. My grandmother had always sat on the stool to conduct her lengthy phone conversations, with a pad and pencil handy. I missed her every day. But at the moment I had no room in my emotional palette for grief, or even nostalgia. I looked in my little address book for the number of Fangtasia, the vampire bar in Shreveport that provided Eric's principal income and served as the base of his operations, which I understood were far wider in scope. I didn't know how wide or what these other moneymaking projects were, and I didn't especially want to know.

I'd seen in the Shreveport paper that Fangtasia, too, had planned a big bash for the evening—"Begin Your New Year with a Bite"—so I knew someone would be there. While the phone was ringing, I swung open the refrigerator and got out a bottle of blood for Eric. I popped it in the microwave and set the timer. He followed my every move with anxious eyes.

"Fangtasia," said an accented male voice.

"Chow?"

"Yes, how may I serve you?" He'd remembered his phone persona of sexy vampire just in the nick of time.

"It's Sookie."

"Oh," he said in a much more natural voice. "Listen, Happy New Year, Sook, but we're kind of busy here."

"Looking for someone?"

There was a long, charged silence.

"Wait a minute," he said, and then I heard nothing.

"Pam," said Pam. She'd picked up the receiver so silently that I jumped when I heard her voice.

"Do you still have a master?" I didn't know how much I could say over the phone. I wanted to know if she'd been the one who'd put Eric in this state, or if she still owed him loyalty.

"I do," she said steadily, understanding what I wanted to know. "We are under . . . we have some problems."

I mulled that over until I was sure I'd read between the lines. Pam was telling me that she still owed Eric her allegiance, and that Eric's group of followers was under some kind of attack or in some kind of crisis.

I said, "He's here." Pam appreciated brevity.

"Is he alive?"

"Yep."

"Damaged?"

"Mentally."

A *long* pause, this time.

"Will he be a danger to you?"

Not that Pam cared a whole hell of a lot if Eric decided to drain me dry, but I guess she wondered if I would shelter Eric. "I don't think so at the moment," I said. "It seems to be a matter of memory."

"I hate witches. Humans had the right idea, burning them at the stake."

Since the very humans who had burned witches would have been delighted to sink that same stake into vampire hearts, I found that a little amusing—but not very, considering the hour. I immediately forgot what she'd been talking about.

"Tomorrow night, we'll come," she said finally. "Can you keep him this day? Dawn's in less than four hours. Do you have a safe place?"

"Yes. But you get over here at nightfall, you hear me? I don't want to get tangled up in your vampire shit again." Normally, I don't speak so bluntly; but like I say, it was the tail end of a long night.

"We'll be there."

We hung up simultaneously. Eric was watching me with unblinking blue eyes. His hair was a snarly tangled mess of blond waves. His hair is the exact same color as mine, and I have blue eyes, too, but that's the end of the similarities.

I thought of taking a brush to his hair, but I was just too weary.

"Okay, here's the deal," I told him. "You stay here the rest of the night and tomorrow, and then Pam and them'll come get you tomorrow night and let you know what's happening."

"You won't let anyone get in?" he asked. I noticed he'd finished the blood, and he wasn't quite as paper white as he'd been, which was a relief.

"Eric, I'll do my best to keep you safe," I said, quite gently. I rubbed my face with my hands. I was going to fall asleep on my feet. "Come on," I said, taking his hand. Clutching the afghan with the other hand, he trailed down the hall after me, a snow white giant in tiny red underwear.

My old house has been added onto over the years, but it hasn't ever been more than a humble farmhouse. A second story was added around the turn of the century, and two more bedrooms and a walk-in attic are upstairs, but I seldom go up there anymore. I keep it shut off, to save money on electricity. There are two bedrooms downstairs, the smaller one I'd used until my grandmother died and her large one across the hall from it. I'd moved into the large one after her death. But the hidey-hole Bill had built was in the smaller bedroom. I led Eric in there, switched on the light, and made sure the blinds were closed and the curtains drawn across them. Then I opened the door of the closet, removed its few contents, and pulled back the flap of carpet that covered the closet floor, exposing the trapdoor. Underneath was a light-tight space that Bill had built a few months before, so that he could stay over during the day or use it as a hiding place if his own home was unsafe. Bill liked having a bolt-hole, and I was sure he had some that I didn't know about. If I'd been a vampire (God forbid), I would have, myself.

I had to wipe thoughts of Bill out of my head as I showed my reluctant guest how to close the trapdoor on top of him and that the flap of carpet would fall back into place. "When I get up, I'll put the stuff back in the closet so it'll look natural," I reassured him, and smiled encouragingly.

"Do I have to get in now?" he asked.

Eric, making a request of me: The world was really turned upside-down. "No," I said, trying to sound like I was concerned. All I could think of was my bed. "You don't have to. Just get in before sunrise. There's no way you could miss that, right? I mean, you couldn't fall asleep and wake up in the sun?"

He thought for a moment and shook his head. "No," he said. "I know that can't happen. Can I stay in the room with you?"

Oh, God, *puppy dog eyes*. From a six-foot-five an-cient Viking vampire. It was just too much. I didn't have enough energy to laugh, so I just gave a sad lit-tle snigger. "Come on," I said, my voice as limp as my legs. I turned off the light in that room, crossed the hall, and flipped on the one in my own room, yellow and white and clean and warm, and folded down the bedspread and blanket and sheet. While Eric sat forlornly in a slipper chair on the other side of the bed, I pulled off my shoes and socks, got a nightgown out of a drawer, and retreated into the bathroom. I was out in ten minutes, with clean teeth and face and swathed in a very old, very soft flannel nightgown that was cream-colored with blue flowers scattered around. Its ribbons were raveled and the ruffle around the bottom was pretty sad, but it suited me just fine. After I'd switched off the lights, I remembered my hair was still up in its usual ponytail, so I pulled out the band that held it and I shook my head to make it fall loose. Even my scalp seemed to relax, and I sighed with bliss.

As I climbed up into the high old bed, the large fly in my personal ointment did the same. Had I actually told him he could get in bed with me? Well, I decided, as I wriggled down under the soft old sheets and the blanket and the comforter, if Eric had designs on me, I was just too tired to care.

"Woman?"

"Hmmm?"

"What's your name?"

"Sookie. Sookie Stackhouse."

"Thank you, Sookie."

"Welcome, Eric."

Because he sounded so lost—the Eric I knew had never been one to do anything other than assume others should serve him—I patted around under the covers for his hand. When I found it, I slid my own over it. His palm was turned up to meet my palm, and his fingers clasped mine.

And though I would not have thought it was possible to go to sleep holding hands with a vampire, that's exactly what I did.

From the *New York Times* bestselling author
of *Daemons Are Forever*

SIMON R. GREEN

The Spy Who Haunted Me

Eddie Drood's evil-stomping skills have come to the attention of
the legendary Alexander King, Independent Agent extraordinaire.
The best of the best, King spent a lifetime working for anyone and
everyone, doing anything and everything, for the right price. Now
he's on his deathbed and looking to bestow all of his secrets on a
successor, provided he or she wins a contest to solve the world's
greatest mysteries. Eddie has to win, because King holds the most
important secret of all to the Droods: the identity of the traitor in
their midst...

Now available from Roc!

M545T0709

**Explore the outer reaches
of imagination—don't miss these authors
of dark fantasy and urban noir that take you
to the edge and beyond.**

Patricia Briggs	Karen Chance	Anne Bishop
Simon R. Green	Caitlin R. Kiernan	Janine Cross
Jim Butcher	Rachel Caine	Sarah Monette
Kat Richardson	Glen Cook	Douglas Clegg

penguin.com

M15G0907